S E A M A N

THE DOG WHO EXPLORED THE WEST WITH LEWIS & CLARK

GAIL LANGER KARWOSKI

Illustrated by
James Watling

PEACHTREE

ATLANTA

For Chester,
who encourages me as I paddle up this river of words.
—GLK

A Peachtree Junior Publication

Published by
PEACHTREE PUBLISHERS, LTD.
494 Armour Circle NE
Atlanta, Georgia 30324

www.peachtree-online.com

Text © 1999 by Gail Langer Karwoski
Cover and text illustrations © 1999 by James Watling

Book design by Loraine M. Balcsik
Composition by Melanie M. McMahon

Manufactured in the United States of America

10 9 8 7 6 5 4 3

Library of Congress Cataloging-in-Publication Data

Karwoski, Gail, 1949–
    Seaman : the dog who explored the west with Lewis and Clark / by Gail Karwoski. -- 1st ed.
        p. cm.
    Summary: Seaman, a Newfoundland, proves his value as a hunter, navigator, and protector while serving with the Corps of Discovery when it explores the West under the leadership of Lewis and Clark.
        ISBN 1-56145-190-8
        1. Lewis and Clark Expedition (1804–1806)--Juvenile fiction. [1. Lewis and Clark Expedition (1804–1806)--Fiction. 2. West (U.S.)--Discovery and exploration--Fiction. 3. Explorers--Fiction. 4. Dogs--Fiction.] I. Watling, James, ill. II. Title.
    PZ7.K153Se 1999
    [Fic]--dc21
                                                            98-43056
                                                                CIP
                                                                AC

Acknowledgments

This book, like the Lewis and Clark Expedition, is a product of the skill and enthusiasm of many people. Any inaccuracies are mine, but these have been reduced as a result of the suggestions of two helpful and knowledgeable individuals.

Jay Rasmussen reviewed the story for historical accuracy. A founding member of Oregon's Lewis & Clark Trail Heritage Foundation, Mr. Rasmussen works with the National Lewis & Clark Bicentennial Council and maintains a list of websites about the expedition ("Lewis and Clark on the Information Superhighway" www.vpds.wsu.edu/LCExpedition/Resources/). Judi Adler advised us on Seaman's likely behaviors and actions. The co-owner of Sweetbay Newfoundlands, Ms. Adler is an internationally recognized trainer of working Newfoundlands and frequently demonstrates her dogs at Fort Clatsop's Seaman Day and other events.

The members of my writers' group (the Four at Five), Lori Hammer, Wanda Langley, and Bettye Stroud, evaluated various stages of the manuscript. A good friend and teaching colleague, Joyce Henson, read early drafts of the story to her students at Malcom Bridge Elementary School in Oconee County and shared the children's reactions with me. Two Newfoundland owners invited me to do "hands-on" studies of their dogs, and I thank Beverly and John Cusac, the presidents of the Southeastern Newfoundland Club, and Joan Crile Foster, co-owner of Halirock Kennel, for providing inspiration.

The folks at Peachtree Publishers, Ltd., have been both patient and painstaking with this project—Amy Sproull and Vicky Holifield made many helpful suggestions. Finally, and especially, I owe a *huge* thanks to my editor, Sarah Helyar Smith, who has devoted herself to this project in her belief that young readers deserve great stories crafted with care and love.

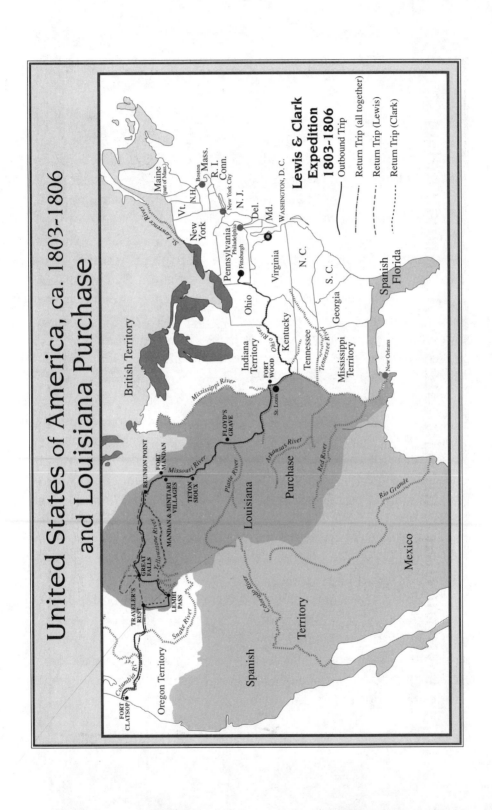

United States of America, ca. 1803-1806 and Louisiana Purchase

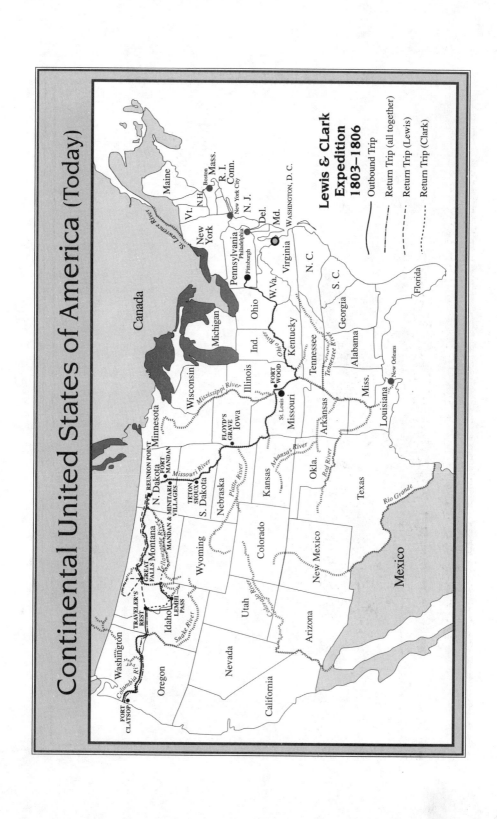

TABLE OF CONTENTS

CHAPTER ONE

N
W ⊕ E
S

A DUCK, A DOG, AND A DEAL

Pittsburgh—August, 1803

The huge black dog trotted cheerfully beside his owner. His long fur ruffled in the summer breeze blowing off the river. He held his head high to sniff the air. A hunter was standing on the riverbank ahead, just at the point where two rivers flowed together to form the Ohio River. The hunter's smell was unfamiliar—starched cotton shirt, new leather boots. The dog watched the stranger closely.

As soon as his owner stopped walking, the dog sat down. "Good job," his owner said, smiling. "When I stop walking, you sit." He stroked the dog's fur. "Nobody has to teach you manners, do they? They come natural to you."

The dog studied his owner's face, waiting for a command. But his owner was looking at the hunter on the riverbank. The dog followed his owner's gaze. The hunter raised his long rifle and aimed at a flock of ducks on the water.

Crack! The hunter fired and the ducks squawked and flew in a panic downriver. One duck floated limp on the water.

The dog's owner chuckled. "Let's have a little fun with that city fellow," he said as he slipped the rope off the dog's collar. "Get it!" he said.

Instantly, the dog bounded toward the water. He leaped into the river and swam to the limp duck. Picking up the duck in his mouth, the dog wheeled around and swam back toward the shore.

Grinning, his owner admired the dog's performance. The dog's spread forepaws stroked through the water like paddles. This dog was a natural swimmer. He moved with the grace of a finned creature.

When the dog climbed onto the riverbank, he shook off and trotted back, duck in mouth. Sitting in front of his owner, he waited for him to take the duck.

The hunter watched, astonished. He strode over to the dog's owner, his cheeks red with anger. "What is the meaning of this, sir?" he demanded. "Why did you send your dog to snatch the duck I just shot?"

The dog's owner put his hands on his hips and laughed. Of course, he never intended to keep the duck. He was just having himself a little joke, that's all. But that hunter looked plenty angry! It was a good thing his fancy rifle could only shoot one slug at a time before it had to be reloaded.

"Thought we'd save you a dunk in the river to get your bird!" he chuckled. He looked at his dog and said, "Give the man his duck."

The dog hesitated.

"That's right," the man said, pointing at the hunter. "Give. To him."

Obediently, the dog walked over, sat in front of the hunter, and waited for the duck to be taken from his mouth.

The hunter hesitated, suspicious. This dog's huge mound of a head was as high as a man's hip. Those powerful jaws could deliver a nasty bite.

"My name's Hanson. James Hanson," said the dog's owner, holding out his hand to introduce himself. "Ain't you the fellow who's come from Philadelphia to pick up a keelboat?"

The hunter's face relaxed, and he shook Hanson's hand. "I'm Meriwether Lewis. And yes, I've come to pick up the keelboat I ordered from the shipyard here in Pittsburgh." Lewis shook his head and grinned. "I have to admit you had me going there for a minute, Mr. Hanson."

Lewis reached for the duck, and the dog gently released it. Turning it over, Lewis examined its feathers. "Seems your dog has a very soft mouth. Except for the spot where my slug entered, the duck isn't damaged at all. I commend you for your skill as a trainer, Mr. Hanson."

Hanson chuckled. "Aye, he has a soft mouth, that's for sure." He patted the dog. "But I can't take much credit for his training. He watched his mama work, that's how he learned. He took to the water right away, when he was still a fuzzy little pup, and he started retrieving by himself. 'Course I did train his mama. Always say she's the finest working dog on the Ohio River."

Lewis held out his hand to let the dog smell him. The dog sniffed the hunter's fingers, and he recognized the familiar scents of gunpowder and river water.

Lewis gently stroked the dog's head. The fur was dense and soft as velvet. "He's a handsome animal, Mr. Hanson. Is he a Newfoundland?"

"He's a Newfoundland, all right. Best dog a man can have on the water!" Hanson declared proudly.

Brushing his sandy hair from his eyes, Lewis studied the dog. Standing stiffly, with his legs ever so slightly bowed, Lewis held his chin in his hand. The way he stood, so straight, reminded Hanson of a soldier.

Finally, Lewis spoke. "Is this a young dog, Mr. Hanson?"

"He's about a year old," Hanson answered. "But if you're asking if this dog's for sale, I'm afraid I can't oblige you. He's been promised to a fellow who's having a ship built here in Pittsburgh. A seagoing ship!" Hanson smiled. "I figure a dog that works this good on the river deserves the chance to work a seagoing ship."

The dog looked back and forth at the men's faces as they talked. He panted quietly, the tip of his pink tongue sticking out.

"I'd be glad to do business with you, though," Hanson added in a friendly voice. "I've bred this dog's mama to the same sire. Every one of his pups is a fine, healthy animal. Full-blooded Newfoundlands, they are. The new litter will be ready come fall. I'd be pleased to save one of the pups for you."

Suddenly Lewis spoke in a rush of words. "Mr. Hanson, would you be persuaded to part with this dog if I told you that I was also about to travel to the sea?"

Hanson looked skeptical. "Didn't you say you came to Pittsburgh to pick up a keelboat?"

Lewis nodded.

"A keelboat ain't no seagoing vessel," Hanson said. "It's made for river travel. For taking supplies up a river."

"What if I told you that I plan to take my keelboat upriver to the sea?"

"Mr. Lewis, I wasn't born yesterday!" Hanson exclaimed. "Ain't no way to get to the sea from Pittsburgh by going upriver. To get to the sea, you go down the Ohio to its mouth, then you go down the Mississippi River to the Atlantic Ocean."

Lewis paused. "The Atlantic is not the only sea."

Hanson wrinkled his brow and squinted at Lewis.

"I intend to take my keelboat down the Ohio to its mouth, then up the Mississippi to the Missouri River," Lewis explained. "Then I'll go up the Missouri River to its source in the Rocky Mountains, where I'll look for the Northwest Passage to the Pacific Ocean!"

"I ain't never heard of anyone making such a trip," Hanson scoffed and started to turn away. But something about Lewis's face held him there. Something made Hanson think he was hearing the truth.

"Mr. Hanson, nobody has ever made such a trip before," Lewis said earnestly. "I've been chosen by President Thomas Jefferson to lead the first expedition to the western sea."

Hanson raised his eyebrows and stared at the young man.

"I want to take this dog with me," Lewis continued. "I need a working dog. A dog that can retrieve game. An intelligent dog that learns quickly and can take commands. A dog that stays calm around strangers, but alert to danger. Your dog is just what I've been looking for. But I can't wait for the next litter of pups, because I'll be leaving as soon as my keelboat is ready." Lewis paused to get his breath.

"What do you say, Mr. Hanson?" Lewis continued. "I'm willing to pay your price."

Hanson hesitated. If what this fellow Lewis said was true—if he really was taking his orders from President Jefferson—then he might be willing to pay a handsome sum for a well-trained dog.

"I'll take twenty dollars for him," Hanson announced, "and not a penny less! As it is, the fellow that I've promised him to will be madder than a hornet. So don't even bother to tell me you want to bargain, Mr. Lewis. The deal is twenty dollars or no sale!"

"Twenty dollars, then," Lewis said without blinking an eye. He reached for his purse.

Hanson stood openmouthed. Twenty dollars was more than a man could earn in a month working at a farm near Pittsburgh, picking crops and mending fences from sunup to sundown six days a week! Why, with twenty dollars, Hanson could outfit himself and his five sons from head to foot, without his missus so much as picking up a sewing needle! Hanson grinned at his good fortune. It certainly wasn't every day that someone agreed to pay twenty dollars for a dog! And in cash, right on the spot.

Lewis handed Hanson the money, and Hanson counted it. Then Hanson handed Lewis the dog's rope.

The dog watched the men exchange the money. When Hanson handed Lewis the rope, the dog whined softly.

Lewis sat down next to the Newfoundland. The man's sandy-colored hair fell onto his forehead, and his fair cheeks rounded into a boyish smile. The dog wagged his tail. Lewis stroked the thick, soft fur on the dog's chest, and the dog licked Lewis's face.

"You say you're going to take this dog to the Pacific Ocean on orders from President Jefferson?" Hanson repeated.

"That's right, Mr. Hanson. As soon as my keelboat is ready, I'll be leaving," Lewis said. Hanson shook his head at the wonder of it. What a tale this would make, he thought to himself. Selling a dog for twenty whole dollars to a fellow who was going all the way to the Pacific Ocean! On the orders of none other than the president himself.

Hanson leaned down to stroke the dog. The dog sprang to his feet. "That's all right," Hanson said quietly. "You have a new owner now. Sit."

The dog sat, but his eyes were glued to Hanson's face.

Lewis fastened the rope to the dog's collar. He put an arm around the dog's shoulders and smoothed the soft fur around the dog's ears. "It's okay, boy," he said in a comforting voice. "You're my dog now. I'm going to take you with me to explore the West. You'll get to swim every day. And retrieve game. And hunt whenever you want."

The dog licked Lewis's cheek. Hanson turned to leave.

"One thing more, sir," Lewis called after him. "What name does this dog answer to?"

"Seaman," Hanson replied slowly. Then he shrugged, a grin spreading across his face. "I named him Seaman 'cause I knew he'd be going to sea!"

CHAPTER TWO

N
W — ◇ — E
S

GETTING READY

August 31, 1803, through May, 1804

Seaman stood beside Meriwether Lewis aboard the keelboat, watching the men pull on the oars. The river was low and the keelboat large and bulky, so traveling down the Ohio River was hard work. The hot sun beat down on Seaman's back. He panted, his tongue hanging out of his mouth.

Suddenly, Seaman raised his head and sniffed. He woofed, trotted past the boat's cabin to the front of the keelboat, and stared at the water.

Meriwether Lewis followed, curious about what his dog had discovered. Up ahead, the water's surface seemed to be covered with furry gray balls, each moving above its own small, sleek wave.

Lewis brushed his hair out of his eyes. "Look at that," he said to the men rowing the boat. "Why, those are squirrels! Dozens and dozens—no, hundreds—of gray squirrels are swimming across the river."

Seaman pranced back and forth eagerly.

"All right, Seaman," Lewis said, smiling. "Get 'em." Lewis tapped Seaman's broad back. The dog needed no further urging. With a leap, he splashed into the river.

The boat's crew laughed as Seaman hit the water. On land, the big Newfoundland's thick, black coat looked bulky. But in water, he was as sleek and graceful as a seal. His powerful legs stroking, Seaman swam into the mass of squirrels and caught one in his jaws. He tossed his head and jerked the squirrel's body into the air, snapping its neck. Then he turned toward the keelboat and swam against the river's current with the limp gray body in his mouth. When he reached the boat, he raised his chin and paddled in place while Lewis leaned over the side and took the squirrel. Instantly, Seaman turned and swam back toward the squirrels.

Seaman repeated the performance again and again. A heap of damp squirrels soon filled the prow of the keelboat.

"That's a fine dog!" called John Colter, a lean, muscular member of the crew. He looked at Lewis, a grin on his suntanned face. "Have you ever tasted squirrel meat, Captain?"

Lewis shook his head no.

"Mmmn, mmmn! Makes mighty good eating," Colter said. "Back in Kentucky, we used to hunt squirrel. The meat's lean and tasty. Makes my mouth water, just thinking about the smell of squirrel meat frying in the pan."

The men pulled on their oars eagerly, thinking of the evening's supper.

"All this game out here!" Lewis shook his head as he gazed out over the broad expanse of water. "I've never even heard of squirrels migrating across a river."

Seaman swam back to the boat, and Lewis knelt down to take a squirrel from his mouth. Before the dog turned to continue hunting, Lewis said, "That's enough, Seaman." He reached out to pull the dog onto the boat. Colter ran over to help. The big dog scrambled aboard and shook his long coat. Water sprayed everywhere, and the men ducked.

Grinning, Colter brushed off his face with his sleeve. "Seaman's a great hunting dog, Captain. Eager to please. Happy to work."

my dog…would take the squirel in the water kill them and swiming bring them in his mouth to the boat.

—JOURNAL OF CAPTAIN MERIWETHER LEWIS, September 11, 1803

Lewis agreed. Seaman's willingness to hunt was one more proof he was the right dog for the coming journey.

That evening in camp, Seaman lay beside Lewis, facing a blazing fire. Lewis bit into a piece of fried squirrel meat, and the men watched him chew. "It's delicious!" he declared.

The men whooped and dug in. Lewis fed a piece to Seaman, who swallowed the morsel in a big gulp. Another man laughed and held out a piece from his plate. Seaman hesitated, looking at Lewis. The dog's furry ears were cocked, and skinny strings of drool hung from his lips.

Lewis nodded. Instantly, Seaman scrambled to his feet. He wiggled his way around the fire, collecting hunks of meat and pats from the men.

When Seaman reached John Colter, he gobbled up the meat then licked Colter's ear. "That's all right, fellow," Colter said, laughing. "No need to thank me. You earned this squirrel meat."

Lewis watched his men play with the dog. Lewis had commanded soldiers, and he knew that a dog reminds men of home, of campfires shared with fathers, brothers, and childhood friends. Seaman could take the chill out of the black nights better than a fire. Lewis watched as his men grinned and patted the big dog. He smiled as Seaman licked their faces and nuzzled their hands.

It was only September, and the Ohio River was carrying Lewis and his men to the frontier—the edge of the white settlements. This trip down the Ohio River was really a preparation—a time to hire the men, pack supplies, and make plans. The expedition to the West would begin the following spring, in 1804. First, the group would spend the winter in training near St. Louis, the farthest major settlement in the western United States. After St. Louis, there were a few small settlements, some trading posts, and wilderness—wilderness that stretched farther than any United States citizen had traveled. Farther than most Americans could imagine.

Lewis knew that blacker, chillier nights would come. As explorers, they were going to face unknown dangers. The expedition would take a year or two to reach the Pacific Ocean and return. When the men felt scared or homesick, the dog would help lift their spirits.

~

Along the banks of the Ohio, the countryside was mostly forest. Trees lined the riverbanks, their leaves still green and lush. Days fell into a routine. The men awoke with the sun and ate a breakfast of leftovers from yesterday's supper. They broke camp, pushed off the boats, and proceeded on their journey.

The group rowed downstream each day, struggling to move the heavy wooden keelboat through the shallow waters. Sometimes it snagged, and the men had to lift or drag it into deeper water. River travel on a keelboat was hard work, but it was necessary because the big vessel could be packed with several tons of supplies. The keelboat had a cabin on its flat bottom, so supplies that had to stay dry could be stored inside.

In addition to the keelboat, the group had smaller boats that were easier to handle—two canoes and a "pirogue." A pirogue looked like a big canoe, except it had a mast so it could be sailed as well as rowed.

On September 13, Seaman was riding up front, on the bow of the keelboat. He sat with his face catching the breeze, his tongue sticking out a little, like a pink half-moon on the black background of his fur. Suddenly Seaman raised his head to study a dark, odd-looking cloud in the distant sky. Sniffing, he stood up and began to bark. In a matter of minutes, the sun was completely hidden, turning morning into dusk. But this cloud did not bring rain. It was a cloud of birds! Passenger pigeons were flying overhead in a thick flock.

Lewis shook his head at the wonder of it. *So many migrating birds!* he thought. *What animals will we see out West?*

The skies darkened again on September 15, this time with rain. It rained for eight long hours, soaking Seaman, Lewis, and the men. The smell of wet wood mingled with the smell of wet buckskin clothing. When the rain stopped, another smell appeared: Mildew! Lewis checked a few of the supply boxes and found their contents had gotten damp. What was worse, some of the guns were wet and were starting to rust. Lewis groaned. With rusty guns, the men would not be able to hunt. They had to keep the guns in working order.

When the boats passed a sunny sandbar two days later, Lewis ordered the men to pull up. "This will be a good place to spread out the supplies," he said. The men unpacked clothes and blankets and laid them out to dry in the sun. They took apart the guns, wiped them dry, and oiled them to stop the rusting.

Seaman stretched out on the sand and watched the men work. Soon he began to pant in the hot sun. He waded into the river and swam up and down the sandbar. When the dog hopped out and shook himself, water sprayed on the open boxes of supplies. None of the men scolded Seaman, though. His playful spirit made everybody chuckle.

For the rest of the day, Seaman took turns swimming and lying on the sandbar. He fished for rocks under the shallow water, scooped them up with his mouth, and made a little pile of them on the shore. John Colter picked up a stick and tossed it into the river. Seaman leaped into the water after the stick and promptly brought it back in his mouth. Colter grinned and rubbed Seaman's wet rump.

It took two more weeks of river travel to reach Cincinnati. There, Lewis told the men to make camp. He had ordered more supplies to be delivered to them at this town, and the men loaded the boats. Seaman romped with the men and dozed beside Lewis as he wrote letters. After a few days, they were back on the river, heading southwest.

The men set up camp again at Clarksville, where William Clark was living at his brother's home. The plan was for Lewis to go ashore and join Clark, who would be his co-captain in the upcoming expedition.

William Clark came running down the steps, his red hair blazing in the sunshine. As he shook hands with Lewis, his eyes danced with excitement. Seaman watched Lewis's face open into a smile. He saw him grab hold of Clark's hand and shake it warmly. He understood at once that Clark was important, a man to trust and obey.

Both Lewis and Clark were tall, about six feet, and athletic. Both moved in big, determined strides. They were men in a hurry to get things done, confident men. They climbed the steps and sat on the porch, talking in lively, excited voices. Clark's brother joined them, and the three ate and drank, laughing and telling stories.

Seaman lay down patiently at the base of the steps. When the rich smell of cooking meat drifted to him from around the corner of the house, the dog glanced up at Lewis to make sure he was still talking. Then he got up and went to look for the source of that wonderful smell. The door to the kitchen was closed, so Seaman wandered around the yard. He could hear the men on the porch. Seaman set out to explore the nearby outbuildings.

At one of the barns, Seaman saw a tall, black man at work on some leather straps. The man whistled, and Seaman approached slowly. Holding out his muscular hands, the man let Seaman sniff his fingers. They smelled like leather and oil, with a fainter odor of horse fur and hay.

"Hello, big fellow," the man said softly. At the sound of the man's voice, Seaman took a step back.

The black man chuckled. "Now don't you act scared of York. Look at the size of those jaws you have. I should be the one who's scared to go near you!"

Seaman nuzzled the man's hands. The man stroked Seaman's fur and looked into his deep, brown eyes. "I bet you'd like to play, wouldn't you, fellow?"

York jogged into the yard, snatched a stick, and tossed it. Seaman raced after it and brought it back to York. He sat with the stick in his mouth until York took it.

"Well, you sure know your manners, don't you, fellow?" York grinned. He tossed the stick a few more times, then he walked back to the barn to finish his work. Seaman followed. While York cleaned and hung up the leather straps, Seaman explored the barn and sniffed the wooden stalls. A cat hissed at him and scrambled up a pile of hay. Seaman barked.

York chuckled. He rubbed his hands together and wiped them on his pants. As he left the barn, he whistled at Seaman. "Come on, big fellow." York walked toward the house, and Seaman bounded alongside his new friend.

"Ah, here's York," said Clark when he saw the black man walking through the yard. He waved, and York hopped nimbly up the porch steps. "Meriwether, do you remember my servant?"

"Yes, I remember York," said Lewis, smiling and clapping his hand on York's shoulder. "He's been with you since you were a boy, hasn't he? If my memory serves me, he was a gift from your father, and York's father was a lifelong companion and servant to your father."

William Clark nodded. "You have an excellent memory."

Lewis took a long, careful look at York. Although the fellow was tall and muscular, he was as light on his feet as a cat. Lewis said, "I'm delighted to see you are enjoying good health, York. Mr. Clark says you're eager to see the West."

"Yes, sir," said the black man. "Master William, he likes to see the world. And York goes wherever Master William goes." York gestured at Seaman. "This here dog was wandering around the barns. I haven't seen him before, but he's sure a fine animal. He belong to you, Mr. Lewis?"

Lewis beamed. "This is Seaman, the Newfoundland I pur-chased in Pittsburgh." Lewis turned to Clark as he spoke. "I've been well pleased with him. Although he's a young animal, he retrieves game expertly. He's a wonderful swimmer, and he's also quite the hunter! Why, he caught a pile of squirrels for our din-ner a few weeks ago. Caught them in the water, snapped their necks, and swam right back to the boat with them. We had quite a feast, thanks to Seaman."

Clark squatted, cupping Seaman's face in his large hand. "There is no finer breed for water travel than a Newfoundland, that's a fact," he said, looking closely at the big, black dog. Clark ran his hand over Seaman's square head and broad back. He felt the dog's muscular legs and thick fur. His smile showed his approval. "He's a sound, healthy creature, Meriwether. Steady and good-natured. I think he's just the dog for our journey."

Seaman wagged his tail, and Clark smoothed the fluffy fur around the dog's ears. "He's a big fellow, though. I'll wager he weighs as much as a man. It's a good thing he knows how to hunt for some of his own groceries!"

Lewis and Clark spent the next two weeks in Clarksville hiring more men. Word had spread about the expedition, and many young men were eager to sign on for the adventure. The captains chose hardy fellows who seemed willing to work, rather than sons of wealthy families. They chose young men who were used to liv-ing outdoors, who seemed cheerful and easy to get along with.

Finally, a group was chosen, and the boats were loaded. On October 26, the men pushed off. They headed downstream with the Ohio River's current. The weather was fine. On November 11, they reached Fort Massac, where they hired a woodsman who knew some Indian languages.

They proceeded on. Three days later, the group made camp at the mouth of the Ohio River, at the place where it flows into the Mississippi, and stayed there a week. Lewis wasn't feeling well—he had chills and fever—and Seaman stayed close to him as he rested in camp. But when the hunting parties went out to bring back game, John Colter asked permission to take Seaman.

Lewis agreed. "Yes, by all means," he told Colter. "Seaman can use the exercise. And he's awfully good at retrieving game." Lewis stroked the dog's fur. "Go ahead, Seaman."

Seaman stood up, but he hesitated, looking at Lewis.

"Go, Seaman," Lewis said, and he pointed at Colter. "Go with Colter."

Seaman wagged his tail and ran off beside Colter.

As soon as he was feeling better, Lewis began teaching Clark to pinpoint their location by measuring latitude and longitude. The angle of the sun's shadow had to be recorded at midday, and at night the position of the moon and stars was measured. The readings could only be taken in clear weather. Although making these measurements was difficult and time-consuming, it was important because the expedition would be going into lands that had never been mapped. As the explorers traveled westward, the captains would take measurements every day or two. When the expedition returned, mapmakers would be able to draw maps of the Northwest using this information and the captains' written reports.

The captains took the night measurements after their men had gone to sleep. They used a special instrument, recording every few minutes for an hour or so. Lewis taught Clark how to identify the stars and read the instrument. Together, the pair practiced, one calling out numbers for the other to record.

During their evening practice sessions, Seaman lay beside Lewis and watched the captains' faces. These men were delighted by each other's company. They were so eager to begin their adventure that excitement could be read in the tone of their voices, the set of their jaws, and the spring in their steps. Their mood was contagious—everybody in the camp felt it, even calm-natured Seaman.

On the afternoon of November 16, Lewis left one of the men in charge of the camp and whistled to Seaman. The dog hopped into the pirogue. Clark pushed off, and the two captains rowed to the western side of the Mississippi River to record the river's width. They pulled the boat onto the bank and hiked through the woods. When they approached a nearby Indian camp, some of the natives strolled over to chat. Seaman sat patiently at Lewis's side as they talked.

One of the Indians held out his hand for Seaman to smell. The dog did not growl, and the Indian patted Seaman. He nodded at Lewis and said, "Big dog."

Lewis smiled. He was proud of Seaman, so he wanted to show off. "Watch," he said, and he tossed a stick for Seaman to retrieve. The dog fetched the stick and sat at Lewis's feet. Lewis took the stick and showed it to the Indian. "No teeth marks," he said, displaying the smooth bark.

The Indian nodded again. He pointed to a pile of pelts. "Three," he said. "Three skins. Good dog. We trade. All beaver skins, very warm. All three for one dog."

The smile faded from Lewis's face, and he turned quite pale. "No trade," he said. "I bought this dog for our expedition. He's worth a lot more than three beaver skins."

The Indian looked at the pile of pelts as if considering how many he should offer.

"No trade," Lewis repeated. He turned to Clark. "Let's go."

As the men strode away from the Indian camp, Lewis spoke in an edgy voice. "Three beaver skins! Did the fellow really think I would take three beaver skins for my dog? Why, I paid twenty dollars for Seaman in Pittsburgh! A man doesn't choose just any dog to take along on a voyage to the Pacific Ocean. Look at Seaman—he's a magnificent animal. As big as a calf and as docile as a kitten. Strong, too. With powerful legs. He swims like an otter."

"Meriwether, please," laughed Clark. "The man thought he was making you a generous offer. In his village, three beaver skins is probably a princely payment for any dog."

"Seaman is not just any dog," Lewis continued, his words tumbling out. "Did you see the way he handled himself in that village? Not so much as one growl. He never left my side. Sat right down, as patient as a grandmother. Didn't bother the food cooking over the fires. Why, he even ignored the village dogs...."

Clark threw his big arm around his partner's shoulder. "Meriwether Lewis, I declare you would trade me before you'd part with that dog!"

Lewis laughed, his face turning pink. "Well, I prize the animal for his qualifications for our journey."

"Of course you do, man," Clark said, chuckling. "And well you should. But the Indian's offer was not an insult. In his way, he was complimenting your choice of a dog."

~

On November 20, the men loaded the boats to continue their journey. They pushed into the Mississippi River and turned the boats upstream, heading toward the mouth of the Missouri River. After making camp for the winter, they would be traveling upstream on the Missouri for most of their trip west.

As soon as the boats turned upstream, the captains knew they had underestimated their task. The boats were heavily loaded with supplies, and the river's current was swift. Although the men were strong and hardy, they were straining against their oars. Going against the current was so difficult that they had to take a zigzag course. They rowed the boats across the river, heading slightly upstream at each crossing. But this method was terribly slow. The boats only traveled about one mile upstream in each hour.

It was not long before Lewis turned to Clark and spoke in a grim voice. "We are going to need more muscle on our expedition. We need more men."

Clark nodded. He had come to the same conclusion. "I know. But more men means we'll need more supplies."

"Yes, and more supplies means we'll need more boats. And

more hunters to supply us with more game." Lewis frowned.

Clark watched Lewis's face. "It's a good thing we discovered this now, Meriwether," he said calmly.

Lewis nodded. He shook off his dark mood. After all, he thought with a rush, they were about to begin the greatest adventure in the history of the United States! "That's agreed, then," Lewis said, clapping his hand on Clark's shoulder. "We'll take on more men at the army post at Kaskaskia."

The expedition reached Kaskaskia on November 28. More men were recruited. More supplies were loaded. A spot was chosen for winter camp at the mouth of the Missouri River. By mid-December, the men were building Camp Wood.

At first, the winter camp bustled with activity. The men were busy sawing, hammering, and moving supplies. As soon as Camp Wood was complete, the men settled into a routine. Lewis made trips to St. Louis to purchase more supplies, mail letters, and make arrangements. He and Clark talked with traders and trappers who had been up the Missouri River. The captains sketched informal maps of their intended route, based on these conversations.

Seaman went on hunting trips with John Colter. He ran beside the men on their training drills. Whenever York had time, he threw sticks into the river for Seaman to retrieve. One of the younger men, George Shannon, wrestled playfully with him.

~

By the middle of March, the Missouri River was free of ice. The days grew warmer, and the men grew restless to begin their adventure. On the morning of March 31, Lewis and Clark sat together, looking over a list of names. Seaman dozed beside Lewis as the captains talked. When they got up and strode into the open area in the center of Camp Wood, Seaman trotted along next to them.

The captains ordered the men to assemble. Seaman watched as the captains announced the names of the men chosen to come on the expedition to the Pacific Ocean. Each man stepped forward as the captains called his name. These men would be the main party of explorers, the Corps of Discovery.

Twenty-six men were chosen to be in the Corps of Discovery. Three sergeants were announced: Charles Floyd, Nathaniel Pryor, and John Ordway. Nine of the men were from Kentucky, including John Colter and young George Shannon. Two of the chosen men were brothers, two were cousins, and some were friends. A few of the men had been raised by Indian mothers and could speak a few words of tribal languages. Some of the men had traded with the Indians and knew the sign language used by the tribes that lived along the Missouri River. The group included men who were expert hunters, fishermen, and trappers. There were men who could run a blacksmith forge, build with wood, steer a boat, and play a fiddle. Almost all of the men were in their late twenties or early thirties and unmarried, like their captains.

The captains told the rest of the men—a smaller group of about twenty—that they would go along for the first part of the journey. The smaller group would return with the scientific notes and samples of plants and animals that were collected during the first leg of the journey.

As soon as the announcements were finished, the men chosen to be in the Corps of Discovery whooped with joy. They shook each other's hands and slapped backs all around. George Shannon raced over to Seaman and threw his arms around the big dog's neck. At eighteen, Shannon was the youngest man to be chosen. Seaman licked Shannon's cheeks, his tail waving back and forth.

Although York's name was not read aloud, Clark put his hand on the black man's shoulder and said he would be part of the Corps of Discovery. York broke into a little jig, and John Colter grinned and clapped his hands. Barking happily, Seaman romped around the group.

Lewis and Clark watched the merriment, beaming like proud fathers. Soon the Lewis and Clark expedition would begin.

CHAPTER THREE

N

W —◇— E

S

THE JOURNEY
BEGINS

May 21 through early July, 1804

Seaman rushed from side to side of the keelboat, his wet tail slapping the supplies lashed tightly against the vessel's cabin. The river was bustling with activity. Men splashed into the water and climbed into the canoelike pirogues. Their faces glistened in the warm, steady rain as they jumped into the boats. They grabbed their oars and steadied their vessels.

As the explorers readied the boats, a small crowd gathered to watch the Lewis and Clark expedition take off. At last, the boats were ready. The townsfolk gave three cheers. The men on board answered with shouts and cheers.

Seaman squeezed past George Shannon, heaved himself up, and balanced his front paws on the boat's rail. He barked and wagged his sopping tail.

"Hey!" complained Shannon as the dog's tail swatted his face, leaving a smear of mud across his cheek. He wiped his face and gave the dog a good-natured shove. Seaman turned and licked Shannon's nose.

"When will you return?" hollered a voice from the shore.

"In two years' time," shouted Shannon, standing up and waving good-bye. "After we've tasted the brine of the Pacific Ocean!"

It was late on the afternoon of May 21, 1804, when the boats pulled into the Missouri River. The expedition was leaving behind the civilization they knew. From now on, these fifty men would be traveling through wilderness. Their map would be the Missouri River. The only people they expected to see were Indians and a few trappers.

Seaman settled down and watched George Shannon dig a long pole into the river's bottom. As Shannon pushed against his pole, he walked toward the back end of the keelboat, forcing the boat to move forward against the current. Ten or twelve men poled at a time, half on each side of the boat. When they reached the back end of the keelboat, they pulled out the poles and walked to the bow of the boat to begin again.

On that first afternoon, they traveled just over three miles. Clouds were gathering as they made camp on an island. It rained hard all night. At six o'clock in the morning on May 22, they proceeded on.

Traveling against the Missouri's current with the heavily loaded keelboat was difficult. If there was any wind, the men ran up the boat's sail. If not, they had to use muscle-power to row or pole the boat upstream. Sometimes they sailed and poled at the same time.

If sailing, rowing, and poling didn't move the boat upriver, a team of men jumped out and trudged along the shore, pulling the boat at the end of stout lines. These men sometimes had to walk through water up to their hips or waists, and they often slipped on the muddy bottom. Seaman splashed through the shallows or swam next to the men while they waded. He loved to be wet, and the sight of him encouraged the tired men.

Since the current was strongest in the center of the river, the men tried to keep the keelboat close to either shore. But the Missouri's muddy banks often caved into the water, endangering men and boats. Rocks, sandbars, or dead trees hidden just under the surface of the river would snag the boat. The Corps of

Discovery was not the first group to encounter these problems. Traders using the Missouri waterway had complained about how difficult it was for travel, and had given it the nickname "Big Muddy."

Clark usually rode on the keelboat. He loved to be around people, and he was a better waterman than Lewis. As the group traveled, Clark kept track of their distance and recorded it in his field notes. He also sketched maps of their route. To estimate the distance the boats traveled, Clark used "dead reckoning." He picked out a landmark ahead of the boat—sometimes a sandbar, sometimes a large tree jutting out over the river. Then he estimated how long it took the boat to reach that spot and how fast the boat was traveling. Clark compared how long it had taken their boat to travel the same distance at that speed on the Ohio or Mississippi Rivers—waterways that had already been mapped and measured. Each day Clark measured how far the expedition traveled. He hoped to measure the whole journey to the Pacific Ocean. When the Corps of Discovery returned to the United States, Clark planned to give his notes to mapmakers so they could draw a map of North America.

Lewis preferred walking to boating. He enjoyed being alone to observe his surroundings. In the mornings, after the men broke camp, Lewis would whistle for Seaman. Together they set off, picking their way through the lush plant growth beside the river. Lewis might cover thirty miles in a day, his long legs striding briskly through the woods. In the late afternoon, he made his way back to the river to rejoin the boats.

On his walks, Lewis stopped often to examine a flower or pull a leaf from a tree. He collected some plants and sketched others. Sometimes he leaned against a tree to watch an animal or listen to the song of a bird. Many of these plants and animals were unknown to American scientists, and it was part of Lewis's job to find out what kinds of life could be found west of the Mississippi River.

Seaman did not always stay close to Lewis. He bounded off through the woods in pursuit of a squirrel or a rabbit. Usually he found his way back to camp by evening, but sometimes he spent the night hunting and rejoined the men as they were pushing off the boats the next morning.

Of all the difficulties the explorers encountered while traveling on "Big Muddy," the biggest problems were caused by the smallest of pests. Ticks latched onto their skin, and gnats swarmed around their ears and eyes. Clouds of mosquitoes buzzed around them, especially in camp. The men stood in the smoke of the fires to keep off the insects. They smeared thick, smelly bear grease on their necks and faces and hands to protect their skin.

Seaman was constantly rubbing the flying insects out of his eyes and off his nose with his paws. Although his fur was too thick for the gnats and mosquitoes to penetrate, the ticks burrowed through his coat to reach his warm skin. These small, flatbodied creatures buried their heads into his hide and feasted on

...Capt. Lewis went out above the river & proceeded on one mile, finding the Countrey rich, the wedes & Vines So thick & high...

—Journal of Captain William Clark, June 8, 1804

his blood. They swelled up to the size of acorns if he couldn't reach them with his claws or his teeth.

Sitting by the campfire in the evenings, George Shannon ran his hands through Seaman's fur, searching for ticks. "Hold still, Seaman," he said. "Fourteen ticks I've picked off you. And I've only gotten as far as your chest. You're a regular pasture for these varmints!"

Seaman rolled onto his side and stretched out his long legs. When Shannon talked to him, his tail thumped against the ground. Shannon picked off the ticks one by one and flicked them into the fire. The blood-swollen ticks popped as the flames consumed them.

In a little over a month, the explorers traveled about four hundred miles up the Missouri River. On the morning of July 4, the men celebrated America's twenty-eighth birthday by firing their swivel gun, a cannon mounted on the keelboat. Seaman barked and the men cheered. That afternoon, they pulled up the boats at

S E A M A N

the mouth of a creek and named it Independence Creek in honor of the holiday. At sunset, they fired the cannon once again.

The next evening, the keelboat got caught in a tangle of drift-wood. The men soon spotted the source of the driftwood—a beaver lodge. Clark ordered the boats to pull in for evening camp. If the hunters could shoot some beavers, there would be a feast around the evening campfires. Beaver meat is tasty, and the men considered beaver tail a delicacy.

Clark looked around, but there were no beavers in sight. The animals had taken shelter in their underwater lodge when they heard the noise of the approaching boats. Jumping out of the boat, Clark waded to the bank and whistled for Seaman. The dog bounded over, his eyes eagerly searching Clark's face.

Pointing at the heap of wood jutting out of the water, Clark rested his other hand on Seaman's back. "It's a beaver lodge, Seaman. Get 'em." He nudged Seaman, then grabbed his gun.

Seaman leaped into the river. He swam to the edge of the beaver lodge and dived beneath the water. A few of the men picked up their guns and joined Clark on the bank. They kept their eyes on the spot where Seaman had gone under. Soon the dog surfaced and dived again, driving a beaver to the surface. One of the men fired and the beaver vanished, leaving a trail of red on the water. Seaman lunged toward it. In an instant, he had the beaver in his mouth, and he was swimming toward shore. He hopped out of the water and ran to Clark, water pour-ing off his coat. He sat in front of Clark, beaver in mouth and tail wagging.

Clark grinned as he took the beaver. He said, "Good job, Seaman! Get another one."

Seaman sprang to his feet and leaped back into the river to flush out another beaver. The men whooped for joy! The thought of roasted beaver meat made their mouths water. Although game was plentiful and the men ate heartily each evening, their appetites were always sharp.

The expedition had brought along a few horses, and several men rode out of camp every morning to hunt. At nightfall, the hunters rejoined the boat crews at the river, bringing fresh game to add to the evening meal.

On the days when Lewis rode on the keelboat, Seaman sometimes ran alongside the mounted hunters. He retrieved game and chased wounded animals. Seaman could carry birds and rabbits in his mouth. He dragged the larger animals, like deer, back to the hunters.

John Colter loved hunting duty. He was at home in the woods, a skilled hunter and tracker. Although he was reserved around the men, Colter had a way with horses and other animals. He always whistled for Seaman to join him when he hunted.

As soon as he spotted the dog returning, a fat turkey or duck in his mouth, Colter would dismount. "Come on, Seaman. There's a fine fellow!" he called, his hazel eyes sparkling.

Seaman ran to Colter and sat, the game in his mouth. "Look at this fine work!" Colter would exclaim. "Why, our supper is hardly bruised! You make the cook's job too easy, Seaman!" Then Colter would open his knapsack, pull off some jerky, and reward Seaman with a tasty chunk of dried meat.

Each day, from early morning until nightfall, the explorers worked hard. But there were few complaints. The warm, sunny countryside was full of deer. Wild grapes and strawberries grew at the edge of clearings, and purple raspberries were ripening along the riverbanks. The explorers ate enormous helpings at supper— as much as nine pounds of meat apiece—and they slept hard each night. This was a new world to explore, and in the summer of 1804, it was a beautiful place.

CHAPTER FOUR

A DESERTER
AND A DEATH

July 11 *through late August,* 1804

Stooping over the campfire, York scooped out a spoonful of steaming hot stew and blew on it. Seaman sat up, his eyes begging. The delicious aroma made him drool. Two long strings of saliva hung from his mouth, one on each side.

"All right, big fellow," York said, chuckling. "Here's a taste of what I'm cooking." York flicked a piece of meat onto the ground for Seaman.

Seaman scrambled to his feet and snatched the piece of meat. Instantly, he spat it out.

"Now you know better than to grab a piece of meat that came right out of a boiling pot," York scolded. "Weren't you watching me blow on this here spoon?"

Seaman rolled the meat along the ground with his nose, licking it tenderly. York sipped the liquid on his spoon. "I think our supper's ready to eat. What do you think, fellow?"

At last the meat was cool enough for Seaman to grab. He swallowed it in a single gulp and looked hopefully at York.

York frowned. "Now look at that! You swallowed your meat so

fast you couldn't even taste it." York flicked another piece on the ground. "This time, slow down and chew."

While York cooked, the captains relaxed by the fire, their writing desks on their laps and quill pens in their hands. Each captain had an open bottle of ink and a journal to write in. All around the camp, the other explorers sat in groups around fires, cooking and writing, talking and eating.

Lewis looked up from his writing. "You know, William, I'm awfully surprised we haven't seen any Indians since we left Camp Wood."

Clark nodded. "By my estimate, we've come over five hundred miles up the Missouri. There's plenty of game by the river. I thought surely we'd meet up with a few Indian hunting parties by now."

"The trip has gone so smoothly," Lewis said. He looked around the peaceful camp.

"Perhaps too smoothly," Clark said.

Lewis looked puzzled.

"The men have gotten too relaxed," Clark explained. "Trouble never seems to come when you're prepared for it. It's when you forget to keep a watchful eye that problems develop."

During that very night, a man was discovered asleep on his guard duty. That jolted the captains. Anyone could enter an unguarded camp, steal supplies and guns, even kill the soldiers. The men needed to take their responsibilities more seriously! This, after all, was a military expedition into unknown territory, not a vacation trip. Under military rules, sleeping on guard duty is such a serious offense that it can be punished by death. The sleepy guard was put on trial and sentenced to four whippings—twenty-five lashes a night—a severe punishment intended to keep future guards from making the same mistake.

Seaman's instinct was to protect each of the men. But Lewis called him to his side on the evening of the first whipping. "Sit, Seaman," he said. "Stay." His voice was clear and firm.

Seaman sat, but he sprang to his feet when the whipping began. Lewis told Seaman to sit again, and he kept his hand on the dog's head to remind him. Whining softly, Seaman watched one of the men whip the guard's bare back. He could smell the guard's sweat and the blood on his back. Although the guard gasped with pain, the whipping continued—twenty-five lashes.

When the whipping was finished, Lewis strode away from the group, and Seaman trotted beside him. Although every man in the Corps of Discovery thought of Seaman as "our dog," he was Captain Meriwether Lewis's dog first.

~

On July 14, Seaman went hunting with Captain Clark and some of the men. The hunters came upon some elk near the river. The men fired, but their gunshots missed. The elk leaped into the river and started to swim away. Seaman charged into the river and swam furiously. Clamping onto a young elk, Seaman managed to break its neck and haul it back to shore. Clark and the men cheered as Seaman swam toward them with the game.

The expedition reached the Platte River by late July. On the thirtieth of July, the captains took a walk on the prairie. The fertile land that stretched before their eyes seemed endless, the sky enormous. A mild breeze rustled the tall grass.

Seaman romped beside the captains. He sniffed the ground and followed the scent trail left by a rabbit. When he discovered the dried remains of mouse, he nudged its stiff hide. Then he rolled over and over, rubbing the scent onto his fur. Lewis whistled, and Seaman scrambled to his feet and ran to the captains. The long grasses tickled his whiskers as Seaman pushed through them. Like a puppy, he leaped into the air to snap at a grasshopper. The captains laughed and ruffled the fur behind his ears.

They walked until they came upon a pond. Swans were gliding across the clear water. Seaman stood, poised and waiting for the command to dive into the water in pursuit of the swans. Instead, the captains stood as still and silent as the tree trunks. The men's eyes drank in the beauty that surrounded them. They couldn't think of words to capture how they felt.

That evening, as they returned to camp, they were greeted by the smell of fresh catfish frying over the open fires. Lewis turned to Clark and clapped a weathered hand on his co-captain's shoulder. "There you are, man. That expresses it."

Clark was puzzled. "Whatever are you talking about, Meriwether?"

Lewis grinned. "The words we lacked on the prairie. When I smelled this fish frying, it came to me: This land is a feast—a feast for the eyes, the mind, and the belly!"

Clark laughed. "Meriwether, you astonish me! You're as tough as buckskin on the surface. But underneath, you have the soul of a poet!"

The amazing richness of the land continued to unfold before them. In the month of August, the expedition finally met up with a party of Indians.

The Indians visited the explorers' camp on August 2. Using gestures, they introduced themselves. They were from a tribe known as the Oto. With hand signs as well as short English words, the captains managed to invite the Oto visitors back for a meeting the next morning.

The men of the expedition dressed in their military uniforms for the meeting. Captains Lewis and Clark even put on their cocked hats. Before the Indians arrived, the men prepared the camp for company. They drove poles into the ground and draped the keelboat's sail over the poles to provide shade for the meeting.

The Indians arrived about ten in the morning. Lewis gestured for them to sit beneath the sail. Seaman was edgy with so many strangers in the camp. He sat apart from the Indians, but he stayed nearby, so he could watch both the explorers and their guests.

Once the Indians were seated, the explorers lined up and marched, military style—left, right, left, right. "Company, halt!"

During the drill, the Indians sat erect, watching the display. They did not speak or smile or gesture.

At the end of the parade, Clark ordered the men to fire a volley. On command, the men fired their muskets. The loud noise startled the Oto braves. Seaman sprang to his feet and stood, his body tense.

After the captains gave the "at ease" command, they joined the Indians under the sail. Lewis took charge of the meeting, so Seaman padded over to Clark and settled down beside him. While Lewis made a speech, Clark took notes. Some of the explorers had learned to speak a few Indian words when they had been trappers. They knew how to make the hand signs that the Plains tribes used for trading with other tribes. They did their best to interpret Lewis's English so the Indians could understand.

Lewis explained that the land west of the Mississippi River belonged to the United States now. The French had sold the territory in what was called the Louisiana Purchase. Lewis likened the situation to adopting a family, and he told the Otos they were the "children" of a new "father." This new father was President Thomas Jefferson. Lewis said the new father wanted to have a peaceful relationship with all his children. The whites would become the Indians' trading partners, and everybody would grow rich.

Lewis spoke for half an hour. He encouraged the Indians to be friendly and helpful members of their new family. He told them to be peaceful neighbors to the other Indian tribes. But he also warned that if the Otos caused trouble, they would be sorry! He said President Jefferson was "the great chief of the seventeen great nations of America." And he described how powerful the United States was, with trained armies and many weapons. If the Otos tried to fight, they would be punished as severely "as the fire consumes the grass of the plains."

The Indians listened politely. Then their chief stood and made a short speech. He told the captains he was glad they had come in peace. He agreed to follow Lewis's suggestions.

And he said he was looking forward to gifts from his new white father.

The captains gave a few small presents to the Oto visitors: medals, cloth, a little bit of ammunition, and whiskey. When the Indians stood to leave, Seaman jumped to his feet. He stood close to Lewis's legs as the captains waved good-bye.

The men packed up to continue traveling, and the captains discussed their first meeting with Indians. As he talked, Lewis knelt beside Seaman and stroked his fur. "I think it went well," Lewis said. "What do you think, William?"

"I'm not sure how much of your speech the Otos understood," Clark said. "But they seemed friendly enough. I think they were pleased with our gifts."

As the men pushed the boats into the river, they joked and laughed like schoolboys at recess. They had finally met some Indians, and things had gone so well! Colter peeled off his shirt and threw himself into the water. He called Seaman to swim with him, and the two splashed around until the keelboat crew yelled for Colter to take his pole.

A few days after the meeting with the Otos, on the eighth of August, Lewis was sitting in the cabin of the keelboat with his samples spread out around him. Seaman sat beside him, sniffing the collection of dried leaves and animal skeletons. Lewis weighed and measured, sketched and noted. As he wrote, he asked himself how he could describe what he was finding in the wilderness so that scientists living in a big city like Philadelphia would be able to understand.

Suddenly, Seaman stood up. The smell of birds was blowing off the river. He stuck his head out of the cabin and woofed. The smell was very strong.

"Cap'n, take a look at this!" called one of the men in the front of the boat.

Lewis rushed to the bow of the keelboat, with Seaman at his heels. The river had turned into a gigantic dessert! It looked like it was covered with whipped cream, all white and frothy! Actually, their boats were moving into a sea of white feathers that stretched as far as Lewis could see. Three miles passed, and still the feathers blanketed the surface of the water, seventy yards wide!

Finally, a sandbar came into view. Lewis whistled, astonished. So many white pelicans stood on the sandbar that the ground beneath their feet could not be seen! The skinny, long-legged birds were poking their beaks into their feathers to clean themselves. As they preened, some of their feathers fell out and blew onto the water.

As the keelboat approached the sandbar, mosquitoes swarmed, thick as fog. Seaman rubbed them out of his eyes with his paws, shaking his head to dislodge the pests. He lay down and covered his eyes and nose with his front legs. The men ran their sleeves across their faces and beat the air around them to drive off the insects.

Fascinated, Lewis watched the pelicans until the keelboat rounded a bend in the river. "Come on, fellow," he said, ruffling Seaman's fur. "It seems we have our work cut out for us. Just as I thought we were caught up with our field notes, we have a new wonder to describe for the scientists back in Philadelphia." He strode back into the boat's cabin, thinking about how he could make his words convey a picture of a sandbar coated with pelicans and a river white with their feathers.

The expedition faced its first serious problems soon after the sighting of the pelicans. First, one of the privates requested permission to return to an earlier camp to get his knife, which he claimed he had left behind by accident. When the private did not return in a few days, the captains began to suspect he had deserted. They examined his bags and found he had taken all his belongings. Quickly, they sent a party to find and capture him.

Ten days later, the deserter was brought back. He confessed: Not only had he deserted, but he had also stolen a rifle and ammunition. As punishment, he had to "run the gauntlet" four times. The men lined up facing each other, and the deserter had to run between them; each of the men whipped or beat the guilty man as he ran through the gauntlet.

Although the private had been chosen to be part of the Corps of Discovery, the captains decided not to keep him in the permanent party of explorers. The following spring, when the smaller group returned home with the captains' notes and samples, the deserter would be sent back. This expedition was too dangerous and too important to take along a man who could not be trusted.

Another problem developed, and this one was even worse than the private's desertion. Sergeant Charles Floyd had horrible pains in his stomach, and he could not hold down food. The pain grew worse, so Lewis made him a bed inside the cabin of the keelboat, and York helped watch over the sick man. Sweat poured off Floyd's forehead, and he clutched his stomach. Seaman stretched out on the floor beside the sergeant's bed. When the sergeant moaned, Seaman licked the man's face.

Lewis had studied treatments for common ailments before the expedition began. He had talked with doctors about medicines to take on the trip. But none of the pills seemed to help the sergeant. Floyd's pain kept getting worse.

On August 20, Floyd died. He was twenty-two years old. Lewis did not know the cause of the young man's death. The captain only felt a great sadness that he was unable to cure his patient.

The Corps held a funeral service for Sergeant Floyd on a hill overlooking a river. Seaman sat quietly, watching the men's somber faces. As they said farewell to Floyd, each of the men wondered how many would die before they reached the Pacific Ocean. Perhaps not a one of them would live to tell about their journey. As they prayed for Floyd, they also prayed for safe passage through the perils they would face. In Floyd's honor, the captains named the place "Sergeant Floyds Bluff."

The expedition kept moving up the Missouri River, but the mood of the explorers had darkened. After the men went to sleep at night, the captains stayed up to take latitude and longitude readings. They talked as they worked.

"We've had two major problems with our men this month—a deserter and a death," Lewis said, his face grim. Seaman padded over to Lewis and flopped down noisily beside him. He nuzzled Lewis's hand. "Just one month ago, everything seemed perfect. What will go wrong next?"

Clark stared at the sky. "We're coming into Sioux territory, Meriwether. We only had fifty men, and now one of our sergeants is dead. I'm worried. The Sioux are a powerful collection of tribes. I've heard trappers say the other Indian tribes are terrified of them." Clark frowned and stood up. "I guess there's no point in guessing how the Sioux will greet our Corps of Discovery. We're sure to run into them soon. Then we'll find out."

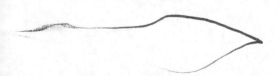

CHAPTER FIVE

SIOUX TERRITORY

August 27 through October, 1804

On the twenty-seventh of August, as the boats passed the mouth of the James River, an Indian boy swam over to one of the pirogues. Some of the men could speak a few words of the teenager's language, and others knew sign language. Soon enough, the explorers understood that the boy was a Yankton Sioux. The captains asked him to bring some of his tribe to a meeting. At last, the Corps of Discovery was about to come face to face with the mighty Sioux!

The meeting took place three days later, on August 30, at Calumet Bluffs. Again, the men wore their dress uniforms and staged a military display. Again, Captain Lewis gave a speech about the new white father and his plans for trade with the Indians. The captains passed out medals and small presents to the Yankton chiefs.

The Indians dressed up for the occasion in buffalo robes and jewelry made of porcupine quills and feathers. Four Yankton musicians played as the chiefs assembled for the meeting. After the soldiers' military display, the Yanktons staged their own display of skill and strength: They organized a competition to show off their boys' ability to shoot with bows and arrows.

That evening, assembled around three campfires, the Indians told stories in song to the music of drums and rattles. The singers acted out great deeds and battles. Each singer, his skin painted with vivid colors, leaped and swirled to make his story come alive.

The explorers loved the entertainment. To show their pleasure, they threw gifts to the performers—bells, small pouches of tobacco, a few knives. Even the captains were impressed with the Yanktons and thought them handsome and well dressed.

Unlike the men, Seaman did not relax during the party. He was nervous around so many strangers—their unfamiliar smells, movements, and sounds. He padded restlessly around the merry camp, his ears alert and his eyes watching closely. He never growled at the Yanktons, but he avoided their touch. He settled down beside Lewis for a few minutes, then moved to sit near Clark or Colter or another of the men.

While the braves danced, Seaman wandered over to York and sat down. The Indians were especially interested in York, because of his dark skin. They swirled close to him, inviting him to join their dance. York laughed and clapped his hands to the music. At one point, he leaped up and danced a short jig. He tried to draw Seaman into the fun, but the dog sat stiffly and wouldn't play.

The next morning, another formal meeting was held with the Indians. This time, the Yankton chiefs made their speeches. The captains gave out gifts of tobacco, but the Indians were not pleased with either tobacco or medals. They wanted practical gifts, such as guns and ammunition, and they said so. Although the Yanktons were openly disappointed with the generosity of their new white father, the Corps could not afford to give away vital supplies—they had a long journey ahead of them. All in all, both groups parted with mixed feelings. The meeting had been friendly and enjoyable, but not completely satisfying.

Soon after the explorers said good-bye to the Yanktons, they realized that one of their men was missing. George Shannon had not returned from a hunting trip. Nobody had any reason to think young Shannon would desert. The captains were sorely worried.

The evening campfires did not seem so cozy without Shannon's songs. Seaman roamed restlessly about the camp. On August 30, the captains sent John Colter, an excellent tracker, to try to find Shannon. What had happened to the youngest man in the Corps of Discovery? Had he been captured by the Sioux?

As the explorers paddled and poled and pulled their boats upstream, they were constantly looking out for Shannon. They kept up with Colter's progress by noting the muddy tracks he left alongside the river. The men also watched for more Indians.

On the seventh of September, Lewis whistled for Seaman. He and Clark were eager to inspect the countryside. The look of the land had been changing gradually as the Missouri River left the Great Plains and moved into the northern plains. The captains walked along the river and gazed through trees at the rolling prairie. Seaman picked up the scent of fresh deer droppings. A herd of elk was just visible in the distance. Clark spotted ripe, yellow plums growing on small trees, and the captains stopped to feast on the soft, delicious fruit.

Seaman wandered onto the grassy prairie and noticed a small squirrel standing on its hind legs. He sprang toward it, but the squirrel seemed to vanish. Seaman twirled, looking for the quick-footed creature. It popped up a few yards away and chattered in a thin, squeaky voice. Seaman darted after it, but it disappeared again. Then, as if by magic, it popped up a few yards to the right. This time, Seaman hesitated. The little squirrel watched him. Suddenly, a second one popped up, its beady eyes alert. Then a third stood up and made a whistling squeak. Seaman turned round and round, watching in confusion as the little creatures popped up all around him.

The captains caught up, intrigued that Seaman seemed to be dancing! Lewis called and Seaman came slowly, glancing behind him at the odd little creatures that were standing and watching him.

Lewis stroked Seaman's big head. "It's all right, boy," he said, grinning. "These animals are not like the squirrels back home. They seem to have escape tunnels, and they slip into their holes before you can pounce on them."

Clark dropped to his knees to examine one of the holes. "I wonder how far down this tunnel goes. I can't see any sign of the creature hiding in here." He stood up and shaded his eyes with his hand to see how far the collection of holes extended. Hundreds of holes stretched out over an area larger than the grounds of Camp Wood. "Quite an army of these little creatures out here, I'd say."

"I'd like to capture one of these animals and send it home to our scientists," said Lewis. "I've never seen a squirrel that makes tunnels like these. I'm going to get the men. We'll dig into one of the tunnels right now."

Lewis came back, bringing shovels and a pole, as well as most of the men. They dug six feet through hard clay following one tunnel, but didn't reach the animal. When the diggers paused to wipe the sweat off their foreheads, York stuck the pole into the hole. "Look," he said, "this here hole goes farther than the length of this pole. We've dug as deep as a proper grave, but we haven't even dug halfway to the end of this tunnel!"

Lewis ordered the men to stop digging. "No use digging up half the prairie!" he snapped in frustration. He ran his hands through his hair, trying to think of another way to capture one of the squirrels.

"Seems we're not having any better luck than Seaman," Clark said cheerfully. "What do you say we give it up, Meriwether? We can just write a description in our field notes."

But Lewis was determined to capture one of the creatures. He sent the men back to the river to fetch a barrel of water. They poured the water into the tunnel, expecting to wash the animal out. That didn't work, and Clark was for giving up again. But Lewis refused to budge without his prey, so he sent the men back for another barrel of water. It took five barrels of water before one of the creatures was finally forced to the surface and captured.

When they got back to camp, Lewis put the little creature in a cage in the keelboat's cabin. Some of the men said these little squirrels were called the "small dogs of the prairie" by French-speaking trappers. But the scientists in the United States had never heard of prairie dogs, so Lewis carefully described them in his notes.

Lewis decided to join the hunting parties to get a better feel for the animal life on the northern plains. He shot his first buffalo on September 8.

The next day, Lewis and another man went hunting. Seaman ran through the brush next to them. As they came to a bend in the river, Seaman raised his head and sniffed. The smell of matted buffalo fur and sweat was new to him. As the huge animals moved, they broke the earth with their hooves, overturning clods of grass and filling the air with the smell of fresh dirt. Seaman pranced around Lewis's legs, woofing with excitement.

Lewis motioned to Seaman to stay behind. The men crept through the brush, approaching downwind of the herd so they could get close before the buffalo smelled them and stampeded. When the hunters broke into the clearing, Lewis shouted, "Get 'em, Seaman!" Seaman bounded after the heels of the galloping animals as the men took aim and fired.

Lewis and the other hunter each shot a buffalo that day. Seaman ran and chased until he was exhausted. As the men quartered the meat and tied it to poles so they could haul it back to camp, Seaman stretched out on the ground, panting.

Pleased with his success as a hunter, Lewis was in a playful mood. He picked up a long stick and urged Seaman to grab hold of an end for a game of tug of war. Seaman ignored the stick and rolled over, sprawling like a tired puppy. Lewis scratched the dog's belly. "We've had a fine day's hunting, haven't we, boy!" he said, laughing aloud.

~

Colter never managed to track down Shannon, but on September 11, the mystery of the missing man was finally solved. As the keelboat rounded a bend, Seaman began to bark excitedly. The men looked puzzled. They had never heard Seaman make this sound. It was higher and louder, more insistent, than his everyday barking. Suddenly, one of the men shouted, "God be praised—there's George Shannon!"

The keelboat pulled up to the bank, and the men surrounded Shannon. The young man seemed astonished to see the boats. He had assumed the Corps had traveled far ahead of him, and he had given up trying to follow. He had lost one of the two horses he had taken with him. His bullets had run out twelve days before, so he had been eating mostly fruit. His only hope was to meet some trappers who might take him back to a settlement.

Shannon was very thin and weak. The men helped him aboard the keelboat, and Seaman jumped in beside him. Shannon sat down, put his arm around the dog's thick neck, and leaned against him for support. Seaman sat very still, examining the young man's weary face. The men handed Shannon some dried meat, and he ate it gratefully as he told his story. Then he rested his head on Seaman's thick fur and fell sound asleep, sitting up! Seaman did not so much as shift his weight until Shannon awoke.

They proceeded on. Over the next few days, Clark killed an antelope, and Lewis weighed and measured it, recording another new animal in his field notes. One of the men killed a jackrabbit, and again Lewis described a new type of animal. They continued to see vast herds of buffalo. Lewis reported seeing three thousand animals in one herd!

The next encounter with the Sioux started out much the same as the meeting with the Yanktons. On September 23, three teenagers swam up to camp. These boys were Teton Sioux, another tribe in the mightly Sioux nation. The captains made signs for the boys to arrange a meeting with their chiefs. The next day, however, the expedition's relations with Indians turned sour. John Colter returned from a hunting trip with some freshly killed game tied to his horse. While some of the men were helping to load the meat onto a pirogue, a band of Indians stole the horse. Colter shouted for help, and there was an argument between the men and the Indians.

The following morning, three Teton chiefs and a group of warriors arrived in camp. They brought buffalo meat as a gift for the white men. The captains gave the Indians some smoked pork in return. Then a formal meeting began. Lewis gave his usual speech about the new white father and the benefits of becoming a trading family. But he soon saw something was wrong. His words were not making a good impression. In fact, the Teton Sioux could not understand anything he was saying. None of the men in the Corps, not even those who had been trappers, could speak the Teton language, so nobody could translate Lewis's speech. As soon as he realized what the problem was, Lewis ended his speech and gave out some medals and other small gifts.

Seaman stood stiff-legged, watching the Teton Indians. Unlike the Otos and the Yanktons, the Teton Sioux did not seem friendly. Instead of sitting quietly while Lewis spoke, the Teton chiefs turned to each other and spoke in loud voices. They gestured with clenched fists and sharp, jabbing movements.

Unable to sit still, Seaman edged closer to Lewis. Finally, he positioned himself between the Indians and the captain.

The gifts did not improve the mood of the Teton visitors. They scowled and their voices became louder. Clearly, they thought they should receive more and better presents.

Clark strode up to Lewis and whispered something. Lewis nodded and motioned for the three chiefs to follow him aboard one of the pirogues. Clark and several men got aboard, and Seaman hopped on board beside Clark. The men rowed out to the keelboat, and the captains, their guests, and Seaman jumped aboard the larger boat.

"Have a seat, gentlemen," Lewis said, in a courteous tone. Then he excused himself and ducked inside the boat's cabin. When he came out, he was carrying a partly filled bottle of whiskey and some glasses.

The captains poured each of the chiefs a quarter of a glass of whiskey. The Indians smiled, sniffed the alcohol, and drank with great pleasure. When they finished, they gestured for more, but the bottle was empty. One of them grabbed the empty bottle and sucked out the last few drops. The chiefs scowled and spoke in angry voices.

Without a common language, the captains could not smooth the situation. Lewis called for a pirogue to come and take the chiefs to shore. This angered the Indians even more. One of the Teton chiefs jumped to his feet, and Seaman stepped forward, a low growl coming from his throat. The Indian froze, glaring at the dog.

"Sit, Seaman," Lewis said firmly, taking a step forward. Lewis exchanged a glance with Clark. Then he gave the Indian a stern look, and the Indian slowly sat down.

As soon as the pirogue pulled up next to the keelboat, Clark jumped aboard and gestured for the chiefs to follow. They refused to move.

Annoyed, Clark called to seven of the men, "Push the chiefs aboard this pirogue! We are going to put an end to this nonsense right now."

The men rushed to obey Clark's order. As soon as the Indians were aboard the pirogue, the men rowed them toward shore. Lewis stayed aboard the keelboat and positioned himself in front of the swivel gun. Seaman stood at his side.

Lewis kept his eyes on the pirogue. When it reached the shore, the chiefs refused to get out. Some of the Teton warriors sur-rounded the boat and grabbed its bowline and mast. The explor-ers demanded that the Indians let go, but the Indians glared and spoke in gruff, defiant voices.

"Enough!" shouted Clark. He stood up and drew his sword. He tossed his flame-colored hair out of his eyes and his cheeks flushed a deep red.

Along the shore, Teton warriors stretched their bows tight and placed arrows across the strings. They edged closer to the pirogue.

"Prepare for action!" Lewis ordered in a stern voice that could be heard on shore. Aboard the keelboat, men grabbed their rifles and knelt by the sides of the boat. Two men loaded the swivel gun, and Lewis got ready to fire.

During one strained minute, nobody moved. Then Black Buffalo, one of the Teton chiefs, yanked the pirogue's line out of the hands of the Indian warriors. He ordered his men to let go of the mast. He jumped out of the pirogue, with the other two chiefs following him. Aboard the keelboat, Lewis exhaled slowly, but he kept his hands on the swivel gun.

"This expedition must and will go on," Clark declared, throwing back his shoulders as he faced the line of Teton braves. "Our men are warriors!"

The Indians could not understand Clark's words, but his meaning was clear from his tone and posture. Still the Tetons held their ground. They stood facing the pirogue, loaded bows in hand, while their chiefs huddled together, speaking in low voices. Clark approached the chiefs and offered to shake hands. The chiefs turned their backs to him. Angrily, Clark turned on his heel and jumped into the pirogue. The boat was pulling away from shore when Black Buffalo splashed into the water, calling to Clark.

Clark ordered the men to stop rowing, and Black Buffalo pointed toward the keelboat. He seemed to be requesting a ride in the boat. Clark glanced toward Lewis, then he agreed. He allowed Black Buffalo and two warriors to get into the pirogue. The men rowed back to the keelboat, and the Indians and Clark climbed aboard.

...3 of their young ment Seased the Cable of the Perogue....I Drew my
Sword....

—JOURNAL OF CAPTAIN WILLIAM CLARK, September 25, 1804

As evening approached, Black Buffalo made signs that he wanted to sleep in the keelboat. Although the captains agreed, they nervously ordered a heavy guard. Lewis slept little that night, and Seaman did not leave his master's side.

The next day, Black Buffalo traveled aboard the keelboat until they came to his village. He invited the captains to visit, and they agreed, hoping to end the tense meeting on a pleasant note.

Seaman stayed beside Lewis as the explorers walked through the Teton Sioux village of almost one hundred white tepees. Hundreds of Indians crowded around to stare at them. When the explorers came to a large tepee in the center, the group stopped. Black Buffalo motioned for them to sit in a circle with some of his braves. The Indians passed around a pipe to smoke.

The explorers noticed many female captives in Black Buffalo's village. One of the explorers knew some Indian languages, and he tried speaking to one of the captive women. She said she was from a tribe called the Omaha. She explained that there had been a recent battle between the Teton Sioux and the Omahas. In the battle, the Sioux had captured Omaha women and children and had killed and scalped many Omaha braves.

That evening, the captains were carried on white buffalo robes back to the central lodge. They watched the Sioux villagers perform a victory dance around a flickering campfire. Some of the Teton men beat sticks on drums made of stretched hides, while their women danced. The dancers wore deer hooves tied to their clothes as rattles. They carried scalps won by their husbands in the recent battle. The women leaped up and down, waving the scalps on the end of sticks. Some Indian men also entered the circle to join the dancing. The explorers threw beads or tobacco to encourage the dancers.

Seaman sat stiffly beside Lewis. He smelled the dancers' sweat, as well as the rancid odor from the decaying scalps. The hair on the back of Seaman's neck stood up, and his leg muscles tensed. A village dog crept up behind Seaman and sniffed his tail. Seaman jerked his head around and snarled.

Lewis placed his hand on Seaman's back. Gently, he bent down and spoke into Seaman's ear: "Steady, boy. My nerves are tight as bowstrings, too. But we must hold our tempers." Lewis was speaking to calm himself as much as to quiet his dog.

Clark whispered to Lewis, "Did President Jefferson give you any instructions for our meeting with the Sioux?"

Lewis nodded. "He wanted us to open up a discussion about trade, like we did with the other Indians. Jefferson warned me about the Sioux, though. He said they were fierce warriors and feared by white traders as well as other tribes. I remember the words he wrote, 'On that nation, we wish most particularly to make a friendly impression, because of their immense power.'"

Suddenly, a young warrior broke out of the dance and gestured angrily at the white men in front of him. The warrior had not received as many gifts as the women dancing near him. He shouted at the explorers, then grabbed a drum from one of the players and hurled it onto the ground, cracking it. Then, as he stalked off, he grabbed two other drums and flung them into the fire.

After he stomped off, two women retrieved the drums and the dance continued. Lewis exchanged an uneasy glance with Clark. He stroked Seaman's back with a stiff, tense hand.

That night, Black Buffalo again insisted on sleeping in the keelboat with the captains. Again they agreed, but they placed a heavy guard on duty. The captains muttered under their breath— were the Tetons planning to ambush them? Neither the captains nor Seaman got much sleep.

Black Buffalo invited the captains to his village again the next day. The Sioux entertained them with another scalp dance at night, but by then the captains were so exhausted they could barely stay awake.

All of the explorers were eager to finally say their good-byes and be on their way. The next morning, Black Buffalo met them at the river with some of his warriors. The Indians grabbed the keelboat's bowline and refused to let go. A line of Indian warriors suddenly appeared along the bank of the river. Black Buffalo demanded some tobacco.

Clark turned to Lewis and said, "He's testing us, Meriwether. If we give him what he asks, he'll ask for more."

Lewis clenched his teeth to prevent angry words from pouring out. Seaman nudged Lewis's hand. Lewis took a deep breath and spoke softly, "We must remember President Jefferson's instructions." Lewis looked at Clark. "The Sioux greatly outnumber us. We must try to hold our tempers, William."

Clark frowned, then he tossed a small plug of tobacco on the bank. He yelled to Black Buffalo, "You have told us you are a great man. Show us your influence by taking the rope from your men without coming to hostilities." Clark turned and walked slowly toward the swivel gun to show he intended to back his words with actions, if necessary.

Black Buffalo continued to demand tobacco.

Lewis's patience had run out. "We do not mean to be trifled with!" he shouted.

Seaman watched the faces of each speaker. He kept an eye on the movements of the Sioux warriors who were holding the keelboat's line. Although he couldn't understand what the Indians wanted or what the captains were shouting, Seaman sensed the mood of both groups. The captains were frustrated and angry, and the Indians were ready to fight. The fur on Seaman's spine stood up. A low growl came from his throat.

Black Buffalo insisted on receiving more tobacco.

Lewis threw a plug of tobacco at the warriors who held the boat's line. To everyone's relief, the Indians let go. The captains ordered their men to row upstream, and the men quickly grabbed their paddles.

As the boats passed a young Indian on the shore, Clark managed to get the last word: "If you are determined to stop us, we are ready to defend ourselves!" he shouted. Clark knew the brave could not understand his words, but he was so frustrated he needed to shout at someone.

Both of the captains were tired and irritated. That night, they ordered the men to pull up at a sandbar. Sandbars were the safest spots for night camp since enemies would have to swim or paddle a boat to reach the soldiers, and the splashing would alert the guard.

The explorers ate their evening meal in silence, each man reflecting on the events of the last few days. As soon as the meal was finished, the captains posted guards and went to bed. Seaman settled down between the captains' bedrolls.

As he climbed into his bedroll, Lewis broke the silence. "I don't think we've seen the last of the Sioux, William. We have to pass through these waters on our return trip."

Clark frowned. "In my opinion, the Sioux are nothing but pirates—the pirates of the Missouri River. It won't be easy to establish trade between our country and the Indians if the Sioux control this stretch of waterway."

Lewis nodded thoughtfully. "We need to create a strong bond with the natives upriver. We'll have to urge the other tribes to ignore the Sioux. That's the only way our country will be able to trade with the Indians of the Plains."

The captains didn't speak for a few minutes. Seaman gave a great, noisy sigh and laid his big head on his front paws.

"At least there was no bloodshed," Lewis said at last. "We didn't establish friendly relations, so we can't count our meeting with the Teton Sioux as a success. But at least we avoided a fight."

CHAPTER SIX

N
W ⬦ E
S

WINTER AMONG
THE INDIANS

October, 1804, through April, 1805

Autumn came to the Missouri River. Along the banks, leaves changed from green to gold. As the Corps of Discovery made its way upstream, the boats were surrounded by creatures on the move. The sky was filled with flocks of honking, squawking geese and ducks heading south to warmer waters. Large herds of elk and antelope crossed the river, migrating south like the fowl. A hearty wind ruffled Seaman's new winter coat. Chilly nights killed off the mosquitoes, and the river water sparkled in the clear sunshine.

In early October, the explorers began to see abandoned villages along the banks of the Missouri. A passing trapper said the Arikara Indians once lived in all these earth lodges, but most of the tribe had been killed by smallpox over the last twenty-five years. Only a few thousand Arikaras had survived, and they lived on one small island. The trappers also said these Indians sometimes joined with the Sioux to attack the tribes living further up the river. After their unpleasant dealings with the Teton Sioux, the captains wondered if the Arikaras would welcome outsiders.

The expedition soon reached the island where the Arikaras lived in four villages. On October 8, Lewis took some of the men out to meet the Indians. Two days later, the captains held a formal meeting with them, including the usual speech, military display, and gift-giving. The captains offered whiskey to the Arikaras, but their chiefs refused. Recalling their meeting with the Teton Sioux Indian chiefs, the captains were both surprised and relieved.

The Arikaras gave a warm welcome to their visitors. They escorted the explorers through their villages and proudly showed off their carefully tended vegetable gardens. When the Indians offered some of their harvest, the men rejoiced. For months, they had eaten mostly meat and a little wild fruit—they longed for the corn, squash, and beans that the Indians cultivated.

As the explorers toured the Arikara villages, curious Indians trailed after them, staring. The Indians avoided Seaman, who was much larger and darker than their village dogs. They pointed at the explorers' clothing and beards. But most of the attention focused on York. None of the Arikaras had ever seen a black man. The adult villagers said York was "big medicine." Some of the village children darted between the explorers' legs to peek at this amazing, black-skinned man.

York found the Indians' curiosity amusing. He pretended not to hear the children approach, then he would suddenly turn on them and roar. When the children scattered like frightened mice, York laughed until his belly ached. "Halloo!" he hollered, showing his arm muscles and making loud, growling noises. "Here strides the York beast!" York leaped at some children. They yelped, scurrying away to hide behind their lodges.

Seaman watched the commotion until he was sure it was a game. Then he barked playfully and ran circles around York. "Fee, fie, fo, fum—now the York beast is come!" York laughed heartily at his own joke and stamped his foot to make Seaman run faster.

"Beware!" York howled fiercely at small Indian faces peeping around the sides of the lodges. "York was fished from the blackest depths of the sea by Master Clark! Tamed in the farthest recesses of caves where hairy monsters dwell!" York picked up a heavy log and hoisted it above his head to show off his strength. "Touch the York beast at your peril—his favorite food is children!"

"York, that's enough!" ordered Clark, shaking his head and trying not to smile. "If you keep it up, the Arikaras will take your jokes seriously. We don't want to mislead these kind people."

After spending a few pleasant days with the Arikaras, the expedition proceeded on. By the end of October, the explorers were entering the territory of the Mandan Indians. The captains had heard of the Mandan from trappers and traders, and they hoped to set up winter camp near these Indians.

On the twenty-fourth of October, the Corps met a Mandan hunting party. Some of the explorers could sign or speak a few words of the Mandan language, and the Mandans had learned a few English words from passing traders. After friendly introductions, the chief of the hunting party invited the explorers to his village. Lewis took Seaman and some of the men while Clark and the rest made camp.

Lewis and Seaman walked briskly beside the Mandan chief. The Indian pointed out fields where his people grew corn, beans, squash, sunflowers, and tobacco. When the explorers entered the village, they passed about forty low, circular living huts surrounding a large open space. The most important villagers lived close to the central plaza, which contained a single cedar post and a big lodge. As in the Arikara villages, Indians came out of their huts to watch the newcomers. The little curly tailed village dogs sniffed at Seaman, but he ignored them and stayed close to Lewis.

The Mandans were friendly, and they didn't stare and point at the explorers. They were used to all types of visitors because their villages were the central marketplace of the region. Indians from many friendly tribes came to trade, bringing livestock, produce, and furs, buffalo hides, blankets, clothing, and firearms—even musical instruments! In late summer, the Mandan villages overflowed with traders from the Crow, Cree, Kiowa, Cheyenne, Assiniboin, and Arapaho tribes. American traders from St. Louis, as well as British and Canadian traders from the North West and Hudson's Bay Companies, also journeyed to the Mandan villages.

Back in camp, Lewis described the Mandan village to Clark. "The Mandans are peaceful farmers, just like the trappers told us," he said cheerfully. "They've been trading with white people for years. If we build our winter camp near here, we'll get along fine with our neighbors."

Lewis was in a great mood. He tossed a stick for Seaman to retrieve. When the dog brought it back, Lewis snatched it and hid it behind his back. Seaman lowered his head and front paws and barked, his rear end sticking up and his tail wagging. Lewis laughed and tickled Seaman's whiskers with the stick, then he rolled the dog onto his back and rubbed his belly. Seaman wiggled away and bounded around the captains, barking happily.

"The Mandans seem friendly and helpful," Lewis continued, his enthusiasm bursting through his words. "I think they have enough corn for their people and for trading with us during the winter." Lewis tossed the stick again, and Seaman pounced on it.

Clark was holding a hot stone wrapped in flannel against his sore neck. Sometimes he was troubled by rheumatism, and the condition had been bothering him for the last few days. His mood was somber. He waited while Lewis played with Seaman. Then he asked, "How many villages are located nearby? And how many natives live in these villages?"

"The Mandan chief said there are five villages in this area— two Mandan and three Hidatsa. From what I saw and heard, I'd estimate the Indian population at more than four thousand in all the villages combined."

"Meriwether, that's more people than live in St. Louis!" exclaimed Clark. "Or in Washington, D.C., our nation's capital city! How many are warriors?" Clark asked pointedly.

Lewis thought for a minute. "Maybe a quarter of the population, I guess." As he worked out the arithmetic and considered the expedition's safety, he frowned.

Seaman sat down with the stick in his mouth, watching Lewis. When Lewis spoke, Seaman wagged his tail hopefully. But Lewis ignored the stick and looked at Clark. Seaman stretched himself out with a noisy grunt, dropped the stick on the ground, and laid his chin on his front paws.

"Almost a thousand warriors are living in the five villages altogether," Lewis concluded.

Clark raised his eyebrows and looked at Lewis. "The Mandans sound friendly enough, Meriwether. But remember: We have fewer than thirty men in the Corps of Discovery, and another twenty men in the group that will return to St. Louis next spring. That's fewer than fifty fighting men compared to a thousand Indian warriors! We must maintain a heavy guard until we're very sure we can trust these people."

"Of course," Lewis nodded thoughtfully. "We'll keep to the system we always use when there's a threat. Only one of us at a time will leave our camp. The other will command the soldiers guarding our supplies."

On October 29, the captains held a formal meeting with the Mandans. Lewis gave a speech, the explorers staged a military display, and the Indian chiefs were given small gifts. After the meeting, Lewis had a talk with Black Cat, one of the most powerful Mandan chiefs.

Black Cat spoke plainly. "When the Indians of the different villages heard of your coming, they all came in from hunting to see. They expected great presents. They were disappointed, and some were dissatisfied."

Black Cat did not mean these words as a threat. He was simply explaining his people's feelings to the white captain. Lewis listened quietly and spoke in a calm, reassuring voice. He remembered his recent discussion with Clark. The explorers would be surrounded by thousands of Indians for the winter months. They all needed to stay calm and try to understand each other.

The Corps began building their winter quarters on November 2, 1804. They chose a spot on the eastern side of the Missouri, near the mouth of the Knife River. The location offered plenty of fresh water, wood, and game. It was across the river from one of the Mandan villages, so trading with the Indians would be easy. The men felled heavy trees to construct the walls of the fort, which they laid out in a great triangle, with rows of huts inside the stockade. They designed the fort to resist attacks, with eighteen-foot walls, a sentry post, and the keelboat's swivel gun mounted as a cannon.

From the first days of construction, Indians came to see Fort Mandan. They were intrigued by such a large structure. Curious Indians hung around all day and slept in the explorers' camp at night. The captains worried about security with Indians coming and going so casually. But as the days passed peacefully, the captains relaxed. Before long, all the explorers considered the neighboring Indians their friends. The soldiers began to visit the Mandan and Hidatsa villages, often spending the night sleeping in the Indian huts.

Seaman, like the captains, eyed the Indian visitors suspiciously at first. He snapped at the Indian dogs if they came too close. But as the days passed, and the explorers accepted the Indians as friends, Seaman allowed visitors to stroke his fur. He recognized the squaws who offered him chunks of dried meat. He exchanged greeting sniffs with the Indian dogs, and he sometimes chased them playfully. When he accompanied Shannon or York or Colter to the Indian villages, Seaman loved to play with the children. He crouched close to the ground and wagged just the tip of his tail, so the children would not be afraid to approach him.

Trappers, as well as Indians, came to Fort Mandan to visit. The captains spent long hours chatting with the trappers, trying to learn about landmarks farther up the Missouri River. They sketched maps based on the trappers' accounts. The captains asked questions about the Indian tribes who lived out West, about their languages and customs, and about how they felt about whites. Lewis and Clark took notes on everything they heard.

One of the trappers was Toussaint Charbonneau, a forty-six-year-old French Canadian living with the Hidatsa Indians. He spoke the Hidatsa language, as well as French and some English, and he had Indian wives who knew the language of the tribes living further up the river. Charbonneau offered to come along on the expedition as an interpreter. He even offered to take one of his wives to help translate. The captains were interested in Charbonneau's offer, but they wanted to get to know him before deciding to hire him.

Charbonneau's wives made their first visit to the camp on November 11, when the fort was being built. They brought four buffalo robes to the captains. Both wives were teenagers from the Shoshone, a tribe that lived near the Rocky Mountains. The two girls had been captured by the Hidatsa Indians in a raid, and Charbonneau had purchased both of them.

One of Charbonneau's wives was a slender young woman with braids down her back. Her swollen stomach showed she was pregnant. She introduced herself as Sacagawea, a Hidatsa word that means "Bird Woman."

After delivering the buffalo robes, Sacagawea watched the men building the fort. Her calm, gentle manner attracted Seaman. Sacagawea seemed frightened by the big dog, but George Shannon reassured her by telling Seaman to sit and by stroking the dog's head. Sacagawea smiled, then she held out her hand for the dog to smell. Seaman licked her fingers, then nudged her hand so she would stroke his fur. Sacagawea giggled. She looked at Shannon and made the Indian sign for bear.

Shannon laughed and said, "I guess Seaman does look like a bear cub! But he's as gentle as a kitten."

Sacagawea opened her pack and broke off a piece of dried fish. She held it out to Seaman, who gently took it from her fingers. When the dog did not jump up or bark for more tidbits, Sacagawea knelt and looked into his rich brown eyes. Then she turned to the other Hidatsa teenager and spoke in Shoshone. She said, "I think this dog has better manners than many men," and both young women grinned.

Temperatures were dropping rapidly. November nights on the northern plains were long and terribly cold. But even the freezing darkness brought new wonders. One night, the guard called the captains to look at the sky. What they saw astonished them—the whole sky had become a vast painting! Streaks of glowing light—brilliant whites, gleaming greens—formed perpendicular columns that seemed to float across a deep black backdrop. The natives had often seen these "northern lights," but the explorers were astonished by their splendor.

During November, lots of snow fell. The men stamped their feet as they worked to keep warm. Their fingers grew stiff, so they stopped to warm them under their coats. Every few minutes, they brushed the snow off their hats before it could melt and run down their necks.

But Seaman loved the snow. He romped playfully as it fell. Sometimes he stretched out on the ground, letting white flakes collect on his fur until he looked like a big, white boulder. As soon as one of the men whistled, Seaman jumped up, flinging the snow into a little blizzard around himself.

Fort Mandan was complete enough by November 21 for the explorers to move in. The men eagerly carried their supplies into the wooden huts, relieved to have a shelter against the bitter winter weather. By the end of November, thirteen inches of snow lay on the ground. The rivers froze over, and the explorers and Indians could walk across the ice safely.

The men put the finishing touches on the fort in December. On the seventeenth of December, the captains recorded a temperature of forty-five degrees below zero. None of the explorers had ever experienced such cold weather. Hunters returned with frostbitten toes and noses. Lewis treated the frostbitten skin by soaking it in cold water. Afraid the night guards might get severely frostbitten, the captains ordered the guards to work in thirty-minute shifts.

After the fort was completed, the men had plenty of other work to occupy their time. They hunted and tanned hides to make clothing and footwear. They built wooden sleds to carry supplies across the frozen ground. And they felled big cottonwood trees to make dugout canoes for the rest of their journey. The work kept their bodies in shape and prevented them from becoming edgy with boredom. But winter at Fort Mandan was not simply hard work. It was a time to trade and visit with the Indians—a time to learn about each other's ways.

Hunting parties went out, often spending several days camping in subzero weather. Sometimes, the explorers and the Indians hunted together. Although the white men expected to have the advantage in hunting because of their rifles, they found themselves bested by the skilled Indians with their bows and arrows. Riding bareback, the Indians controlled their speedy horses with their knees. The explorers were amazed that the Indians could aim their arrows accurately and shoot forcefully while racing after stampeding buffalo!

As snow blanketed the grazing lands, game animals became scarcer and leaner. Hunting was even more difficult because of the wolves that ravenously attacked the killed game before the hunters could dismount. Colter refused to take Seaman along on the winter hunts, because he worried about the dog trying to defend their meat and getting ripped to shreds by starving wolves.

Seaman didn't mope when the hunting parties left him at the fort because visitors aplenty crowded into the enclosure. In fact, so many Indians camped in the fort that the men complained about them getting underfoot! Seaman padded from building to building, collecting hunks of dried meat from the Indians and warm tidbits from the cooks. He settled down inside the doorways and perked up his ears as he watched people come and go.

The Indian visitors came to Fort Mandan to trade, visit, and observe the lifestyle of the white men. As the explorers worked, the Indians learned about thermometers that read the temperature. When the Indians peered through an object called a spyglass, they were surprised to see the tiny pinecones on distant trees. The Indians watched curiously as the explorers scribbled on thin sheets of writing paper. The commonplace details of the explorers' everyday lives, as well as their fascinating tools, amazed the fort's visitors.

The captains settled down to their own work, the task of recording the information gathered so far. Seaman often dozed in the small room where Lewis wrote pages and pages. He listened to Lewis's quill pen scratch out neat lines of cursive. In spite of the dim light, provided mainly by fires and candles, Lewis sat for hours and hours hunched over his writing desk. He described what the explorers had seen and encountered. He recorded where they'd gone and the supplies they used. He wrote about the Indians' customs and his own ideas for trading with the tribe.

Sometimes Seaman brought a stick or pinecone inside Lewis's quarters. He would lie down, his "toy" resting on his paws, and watch Lewis's hand move across the pages. After a few minutes, Seaman would get up and bring his toy to Lewis. If Lewis ignored him and kept writing, Seaman might nudge Lewis's hand.

Lewis would say, "No, Seaman. Not now. I'm working." But when he looked up and saw Seaman gazing at him with such hopeful eyes, he often changed his mind.

"All right, Seaman." Lewis grinned. "I need to get up and stretch my legs. But I'm only going to play for a few minutes. Get it," Lewis said, tossing the toy for Seaman to retrieve.

As the winter months wore on, the expedition's stores of meat ran low. The explorers began to depend on the Indians' dried corn. At first, the Mandans gave away their corn or traded it for trinkets—bits of cloth, metal fishhooks, some face paint. But when the Indians realized how much the explorers needed the food, they drove harder bargains. Of course, the expedition could not afford to part with all of the trading goods, since there was a long journey ahead. Finding a reliable winter food supply had become a major problem.

The problem was solved when the Indians noticed one of the explorers working at a blacksmith forge. John Shields had set up the forge to repair some of the expedition's tools. The Indians owned metal tools received from earlier traders, and some of these tools had been damaged with use. The Indians began bringing their broken tools to the fort, and Shields charged for his work in corn. Pretty soon, Shields was operating a thriving business, with several men from the crew helping him to stoke the fire and run the forge. Seaman made a wide circle around the forge because he did not like the loud noise of pounding metal and the sparks flying from sizzling fires.

After several weeks, the explorers had repaired all of the Indians' broken metal objects. But the explorers continued to need Indian corn. So Shields began making new tools, such as axes and scrapers, and sold these to the Indians.

The explorers provided other services for their neighbors. The white men had some medicines unknown to the Mandans. The Indians noticed that Captain Lewis was skilled in doctoring frostbite and other ailments. Indian mothers began bringing their children to Lewis for various cures. One child had such severely frostbitten toes that Lewis had to amputate them to prevent the child from dying of an infection.

By February, when Sacagawea was ready to give birth, Charbonneau and his family had moved into Fort Mandan. Lewis helped her with the difficult delivery of her son. Charbonneau named their baby Jean-Baptiste. All of the explorers had become fond of gentle, intelligent Sacagawea, and they were proud that her baby was born in their fort.

Seaman sometimes sat next to Sacagawea as she nursed Jean-Baptiste. The dog cocked his head to listen to the small, snuffling sounds that the baby made. When Seaman edged close, the infant wrapped his tiny fingers around tufts of the dog's fur. Sacagawea smiled and sang a soft lullaby to her son. Seaman licked her face and gently nuzzled the baby.

Nighttime inside the fort was filled with firelight, music, dancing, and friendly company. Some of the explorers had brought their fiddles along. One of the fiddlers, a Frenchman named Pierre Cruzatte, knew all sorts of tunes. George Shannon had a fine, deep voice, and he loved to sing while Cruzatte played.

When Shannon sang, Seaman crept close to the young man for a favorite game. Shannon rested his hand on Seaman's broad back and crooned as if he were serenading a pretty lady. Seaman waited patiently until Shannon hit a long note, then he licked the singer's cheek. Shannon would pretend to be drenched with slobber. He would frown and chase Seaman around the fire, waving his fists and threatening to spank the dog. Seaman would scoot away, his tail tucked tightly under his hind end.

The chase would continue for awhile, while the men laughed and whooped, clapping hands and stamping feet. Then Seaman would leap over the heads of the men sprawled on the floor. Finding Colter or York, Seaman would duck under the fellow's arm and bury his head, rolling himself into a round, furry bundle. Night after night, Shannon and Seaman played this game, and it always made the crowd roar with laughter.

All the men loved to dance to the fiddle music. They danced into the night, warming muscles grown stiff with the cold. Sometimes they grabbed a partner or danced a reel; on other occasions they made up their own dance steps and leaped around the floor by themselves. The Indian visitors joined in the dancing and merriment.

York was a great favorite at the evening get-togethers. While Cruzatte fiddled a lively tune, York danced a jig. He moved so nimbly the Indians were astonished. His feet skipped across the wooden floor as easily as water slips between tree roots. Sometimes York coaxed Seaman to "dance" with him. York tapped Seaman's chest and the dog raised himself onto his back legs and rested his front paws lightly on York's chest. York put his hands on Seaman's sides and swayed to the music. Seaman only put up with this for a minute or two before he wiggled away, leaving York to end with a great belly laugh.

As the evening wore on, even the heartiest dancers grew tired. Then the men flopped down, and the storytelling began. While the men swapped hunting tales, Seaman lay with his front paws crossed, his head held high to watch the speakers. When the men told quieter stories about their families back home, Seaman lowered his head and dozed contentedly as John Colter stroked his long, thick fur.

During the month of February, the weather began to change. On sunny afternoons, the top layer of snow melted, then at night it iced over. The men of the Corps of Discovery grew restless to continue their journey. On March 2, 1805, one of the explorers came running into the fort to announce that the ice on the Missouri River had begun to break up. That meant the expedition would soon be able to travel again.

Throughout March, the fort bustled with activity. The men finished hollowing out the new dugout canoes and caulked the older boats so they wouldn't leak. They smoked meat for the journey ahead. Elkskin was dried and stretched into ropes. Supplies were gathered and packed tightly into boxes.

The smaller group of explorers prepared to return to St. Louis with the keelboat and the scientific information gathered in the first eleven months. They loaded the captains' field notes, letters, and journals. They packed the collections of plants and minerals. Hides, horns, and skeletons of animals—badger, hare, weasel,

we had the Best to eat that could be had & continued…dancing & frolicking
dureing the whole day….we enjoyed a merry cristmas….

—Journal of Sergeant John Ordway, December 25, 1804

mouse, and squirrel; red fox, coyote, and lynx; bighorn sheep and antelope—were packed to be sent to President Jefferson and the scientists in Philadelphia. The men carried aboard the live specimens—a prairie dog, a grouse hen, and four magpies—and stored them in the keelboat's cabin. Some Indian clothing was included, along with bows and arrows, a buffalo robe, and seeds for Indian tobacco and corn.

Preparations for travel continued through the first week of April. The captains decided to hire Charbonneau as a translator. Although the Frenchman wanted the job, he asked to be excused from some of the explorers' chores, such as pulling heavy boats upriver or standing guard at night. The captains insisted: if Charbonneau was going to be hired, he would have to do his share of all the work. Charbonneau hesitated, but he finally agreed to the captains' terms. He offered to bring Sacagawea to help him translate the Indians' languages, and the captains enthusiastically agreed. Sacagawea spoke the language of the Shoshone Indians and knew some of the country they would travel through. She would be a living symbol of the expedition's peaceful intentions toward all Indians. Surely, none of the tribes upriver would mistake the Corps of Discovery for a war party if an Indian woman and her baby were traveling with the group!

Sacagawea carried her family's belongings onto the boats, her infant son strapped on a board against her back. The explorers scrambled to help the young mother, and Seaman pranced along the riverbank beside her. When a shirt slipped out of her pack and dropped on the ground, Seaman picked it up and carried it in his mouth to the boats.

On April 7, everything was packed and ready to go. The men said their good-byes to friends among the Mandans. The captains gave final instructions to the group of men taking the keelboat back to St. Louis and waved farewell to them as they headed downriver.

CHAPTER SEVEN

PERILS IN PARADISE

April 7 through May 24, 1805

Bursting with confidence, the explorers plunged into their second season of travel. They had tested their know-how along hundreds of wilderness miles. Why shouldn't they feel confident? Hadn't they struggled all the way up the river from St. Louis and weathered a winter colder than anyone could have imagined? Didn't they have the most powerful rifles ever made? Why, the men in the Corps of Discovery felt they could overcome any peril in the wilderness!

Traveling against the Missouri's current still took strength and patience. But the heavy, awkward keelboat had been sent back to St. Louis, and river travel was a little easier with pirogues and dugout canoes.

Leaving Fort Mandan, the explorers traveled west through the flat country of the northern plains. Small groves of trees lined the riverbanks. Away from the river, there wasn't a hill, a tree, or even a shrub to block the view. Although the prairie soil did not get enough rain to support trees, this was fertile country. The rich grasslands nurtured vast herds of grazing animals—buffalo, elk, and antelope. Immense flocks of birds feasted on the insects hovering over the prairie blooms. Each day, the hunters returned with plenty of game. The men were astonished by the abundance of animal life. For a frontiersman, this was paradise!

Seaman helped hunt for the group's food supplies. Antelope often crossed the river, and although they were very fast runners, they were weak swimmers. The explorers watched both wolves and bears catching the antelope in the water. Seaman copied the wild animals' method of hunting. He would dive into the water and overtake a swimming antelope, bite the back of its neck, push it underwater to drown it, and tow it back to the men on shore. The wild geese were so plentiful that hunting them was easy. Seaman often caught more than his share of dinner.

Since the animals of the northern plains saw few people, they were not afraid of the explorers. One evening while taking a walk, Lewis came upon a buffalo calf. The calf looked up from its grazing but didn't run away. When Seaman came bounding up from the river, the calf snorted and darted close to Lewis for protection. Lewis was amazed when the calf followed close to his heels like a pet until he got back into his canoe. The other men had similar experiences. Sometimes they had to throw sticks and stones at groups of buffalo to clear them out of the way!

On the afternoon of April 13, one of the expedition's boats almost met disaster. Charbonneau was steering the white pirogue when a sudden wind blew up. He panicked and turned the side of the white pirogue against the breeze. The boat leaned over so far it looked like it would capsize, and Seaman slid overboard into the river.

Lewis sprang to his feet and called out directions. One of the men shoved Charbonneau aside and quickly turned the boat into the wind. Others hurriedly pulled down the sail. Seaman treaded water near the pirogue. He kept his eyes on Sacagawea, who had the baby strapped to a board on her back. When the Indian woman scrambled to the opposite side of the boat so her weight would help shift the boat back into an upright position, Seaman swam around the pirogue and stayed close to her.

…a suddon squall of wind struck us…near overseting the perogue….
—JOURNAL OF CAPTAIN MERIWETHER LEWIS, April 13, 1805

As soon as the pirogue was righted, Seaman swam to its side and the men pulled him aboard. When he shook the water off his fur, cold droplets sprayed everyone.

"Stop that, Seaman!" the men hollered, brushing off their clothes. A few of the men chuckled, relieved that nobody had been hurt and none of the supplies had washed away.

Sacagawea covered her mouth with her hand, thinking it wise to hide her grin from her husband. It was, after all, Charbonneau's mistake which had caused the difficulty. Charbonneau crouched in the stern, the back end of the boat, annoyed with himself and everybody else. Relaxed again, Seaman dozed while the sun dried his coat.

Lewis shut his eyes and gave a silent prayer of thanks. Although the boat scare was over in a moment, the memory of it—and the thought of what might have happened—lingered the rest of the day. The white pirogue was the steadiest of their boats, so it was used as the flagship of the expedition's small fleet of two pirogues and six dugout canoes. It carried all the captains' papers and instruments, as well as the medicines, gunpowder, and most of the valuable trade goods. The three men who could not swim always rode in the white pirogue. Sacagawea and her infant son also rode in this boat. If the white pirogue overturned, it would be a tragedy for the Corps of Discovery.

The safety of the white pirogue was not the only concern facing the Corps of Discovery in this new country. When the explorers left Fort Mandan, they were eager to test their courage and firearms against a grizzly bear, an animal unfamiliar to them. The Indians at Fort Mandan had spoken of these fearsome bears, gigantic in size, with silver-tipped fur. During the long winter nights at the fort, the explorers heard many a hair-raising tale about grizzly bears. The Indians said they were hard to kill and extremely aggressive. In fact, the Indians said they prepared to hunt grizzly like they prepared to go to war!

The Corps of Discovery began seeing signs of grizzlies four days after they left Fort Mandan. On April 14, Clark spotted two grizzlies running in the distance. A few days later, some unarmed men caught sight of one. On April 28, the men saw four grizzlies and shot at them. Although one of the bears was wounded, the huge animals ran off.

The next day, Lewis and another man were hunting along the river. In camp, Seaman began to bark, the fur on the back of his neck bristling. His barking was deeper and louder than any of the explorers had ever heard. He dashed out of camp, running furiously after Lewis.

Lewis and the other hunter heard two grizzlies crash out of the brush, and both men fired. The grizzlies roared, and one of the wounded bears turned and ran off. The other wounded grizzly charged. Amazed by the animal's fearlessness, Lewis quickly loaded his gun with powder and ball. Although Lewis had hunted many black bear in the eastern United States, he had never seen a bear charge with such fury!

Seaman raced toward his master, his body pressed low to the ground and his legs pumping as fast as they had ever moved. Before the dog could reach Lewis, both men managed to reload their guns and fire another round at the charging grizzly. This time, the large bear fell to the ground. The air was filled with the stink of bear, the smell of gunpowder, and the tang of fresh blood.

Seaman approached the fallen bear with a stiff-legged walk, sniffing cautiously. Lewis poked at the huge mound of silvery brown fur with his rifle. He was astounded by the animal's size—thick claws longer than a man's fingers and gleaming teeth the size of chess pieces. It took several men to haul the grizzly's enormous carcass back to the boats to be butchered for meat and grease.

Less than a week later, Clark returned from the hunt with a much larger grizzly and an even more frightening story.

"Meriwether, we shot ten balls into this monster!" Clark exclaimed. "But he swam halfway across the river, dragged himself onto a sandbar, and roared for twenty minutes before he died. Oh, the commotion he made! It was enough to make Hercules tremble!"

Lewis lifted one of the bear's huge front paws. "This is a mountain of an animal!" he exclaimed. He spread his fingers to measure the grizzly's deadly sharp claws. "With these claws, he could rip open an elk like he was slicing butter!"

"I bet this grizzly weighs at least five hundred pounds," Clark said, shuddering.

When the men butchered Clark's grizzly, they discovered five rifle balls lodged in the bear's lungs. The animal should have died instantly.

On May 11, another wounded grizzly chased a hunter half a mile to the river's edge. The terrified man shouted at the boats, and a pirogue pulled over to rescue him. The bear ran off through the trees, and some of the men went in pursuit of the wounded animal. They chased it almost a mile through thick brush. Although the bear had already been shot through the lungs, it managed to run a mile and a half before dying!

Three days later, the explorers had their fourth and worst encounter with a wounded grizzly. This time, one bear fought off six men. With six musket balls already in him, the bear chased the hunters to the river. Two of the men jumped aboard their canoe, and four of the hunters hid among the trees to reload. The hunters kept shooting, and the enraged bear chased two of the men off the side of the bank and down a twenty-foot drop into the water. The bear plunged into the river after the men. He had almost reached the swimmers when one hunter finally shot him in the head. It took a total of eight balls to bring down this beast, and the hunters had become the hunted by the time the grizzly was killed.

Now the explorers understood why the Indians at Fort Mandan feared the grizzly bear. The grizzly was the terror of the

West! Lewis wrote in his journal that he would rather fight two Indians than one grizzly bear. In spite of their wilderness skills and their powerful guns, the explorers were finding unexpected perils in this paradise.

The river's unpredictable winds continued to pose a threat. Charbonneau was steering the white pirogue on May 14 when the wind picked up suddenly. Again, he panicked. Unfortunately, both captains and Seaman were on the shore. Although the captains shouted directions, the wind drowned out their voices. They watched helplessly as the pirogue tipped. Seaman leaped into the river and began to swim for the boat.

As the crew scrambled to recover control of the pirogue, water washed over its sides and swept some papers and instruments overboard. In the midst of the confusion, Sacagawea calmly stood and reached over the side of the boat. She snatched the lost articles out of the river. By the time Seaman reached the boat, the crisis was over. The men helped the dog scramble aboard the pirogue. They scooped the water out of the boat and laid out the wet articles to dry.

That day, the captains decided Charbonneau would not steer the white pirogue again. Although their respect for the translator had fallen, they were very impressed with his wife. Sacagawea had stayed calm in every crisis. She had proved herself as brave as any man in the Corps.

The explorers knew how tricky boating on the Missouri was, and they had been warned about grizzly bears by the Indians at Fort Mandan. But the next peril in the wilderness surprised everybody in the Corps of Discovery.

Beavers were plentiful along the Missouri River. Their thick, soft pelts were worth great sums of money in both the United States and Europe. Beaver meat was a welcome addition to the explorers' diet, and beaver tail was a favorite dish. As they traveled, the men shot at beavers or set traps for them. The hunters saved the hides to sell when they returned from the wilderness.

Since beavers never charged at the men, and since Seaman easily retrieved the wounded beavers from the river, none of the explorers considered beavers to be dangerous.

On May 19, one of the men shot at a beaver in the river. As usual, Seaman leaped into the water to retrieve the game. When the dog dived underwater to grab it, the wounded beaver bit one of Seaman's hind legs. Seaman surfaced with the beaver in his jaws and swam toward shore. A red trail billowed out behind him.

With the limp body of the dead beaver clamped in his mouth, Seaman scrambled onto the bank. He began to hobble on three legs toward the hunter.

"Seaman's been wounded!" yelled the hunter.

Lewis came running. Seaman's leg was gushing blood.

The hunter took the beaver while Lewis laid Seaman on the ground. Kneeling beside the dog, Lewis examined the wound. He applied pressure with his hands to try to stop the bleeding.

"Give me something to tie around this wound!" Lewis yelled. "Seaman's bleeding to death! The beaver bit through an artery."

The hunter ripped a piece of buckskin from his shirt and handed it to Lewis, who tied the leather around Seaman's leg above the gash.

A small crowd gathered to help. They lifted Seaman onto a blanket and carried him into camp. Sacagawea tore cloth for dressings, and York gently petted the dog while Lewis worked on his leg. It seemed to Lewis the wound would never stop bleeding!

Seaman's deep, brown eyes glazed over. He twitched from the pain when Lewis cut away his fur and stitched the ragged wound. But there was no need for the men to hold his big jaws shut because he never growled or snapped.

"Steady now, big fellow," York crooned softly while he petted the dog. "Big fellow like you should know better than to let a beaver chew on your leg. Them beavers, they got mighty sharp teeth. They eat cottonwoods for their dinner. You know you gotta watch out for a set of teeth that can chew up a whole tree trunk."

one of the party wounded a beaver, and my dog as usual swam in to catch it; the beaver bit him through the hind leg and cut the artery; it was with great difficulty that I could stop the blood; I fear it will yet prove fatal to him.

—JOURNAL OF CAPTAIN MERIWETHER LEWIS, May 19, 1805

Seaman lifted his head weakly and nuzzled York's hand. His blood had already soaked through three changes of the dressings. Lewis had never treated a wound that bled so much.

As soon as Clark returned from hunting, he was told about the injury. He hurried over to Lewis. "Is he going to make it, Meriwether?"

"I believe we've finally got the bleeding stopped. But he's lost too much blood." Lewis's voice cracked. He looked at Clark, the rims of his eyes moist. "I fear the wound will yet prove fatal to him."

Sacagawea brought some supper to Lewis. While the captain ate, she tried to coax Seaman to lick some salty water. Her baby was strapped to her back as she bent over Seaman, and the dog could hear the tiny sucking noises the infant made. In a low voice, the Indian woman sang a tune her people used to soothe their babies. At the sound, Seaman's tail thumped once or twice. Gently, Sacagawea stroked the dog's big head while she dipped her fingers into the bowl of liquid. At last, Seaman lapped some cool water from her fingers.

All of the men worried about Seaman. George Shannon remembered sleeping against Seaman's broad back after he had been lost and nearly starved. Now he asked permission to sit by Seaman during the night.

Clark urged Lewis to let Shannon watch the dog. That way, Lewis could get some rest. Lewis finally agreed, but he couldn't sleep. He had enough experience in doctoring to recognize a wound that was likely to be deadly. Countless times during the night, Lewis got up to check Seaman. Each time, he was relieved to find his dog still clinging to life. True to his word, young Shannon stayed with the dog all night. He sat with his legs folded, cradling Seaman's big head in his lap.

In the morning, Seaman was still alive. He lay on his side, too weak to lift himself up, but the tip of his tail thumped softly when Lewis came to check on him.

Sacagawea prepared a bed for Seaman in the white pirogue. Shannon, Colter, and York helped Lewis carry the big dog on board. Sacagawea draped a blanket over two sticks to shield Seaman from the sun. Every half-hour as they traveled, she soaked a cloth in cool water and squeezed a trickle into the dog's mouth. Lewis checked the wound at noon—there was no sign of infection. Perhaps his dog would pull through.

By the next evening, Seaman was strong enough to roll onto his stomach and lift his head. Lewis declared the patient was ready for some food, and the men cheered. John Colter had saved a bowl of drippings from the meat, and he held it under Seaman's head so the dog could lap it up. York chopped some meat and mixed it with broth, then fed the mush to Seaman by hand.

That night, Shannon again asked permission to stay next to Seaman, and Lewis agreed. The captain had already decided he too would sleep beside his dog. It would be a comfort to hear Seaman's breathing during the night.

Come morning, Seaman was able to stand up on his three good legs. But Lewis was afraid the dog would reopen the wound if he moved too much. So he told the men to carry Seaman onto the pirogue. That day, the dog rode again in the shade of the blanket as they traveled. Sacagawea dipped a bowl into the river and held it so he could lap the cool water. The men stroked his head and spoke to him while they paddled. At noontime, York fed him a little bowl of meaty mush. If strangers had observed the expedition that day, they would have thought a large, furry creature was king of this little band of explorers and his throne was on a white pirogue.

After a week, Seaman was alert and playful again. Lewis encouraged him to ride in the boats for at least part of each day, until his strength was restored. The men decided they would retrieve their own game until they were sure their dog was completely healed. But Seaman had no trouble swimming. And when he ran, he amazed all of them by showing no signs of a limp.

CHAPTER EIGHT

GUARD DOG AND BACKPACKER

May 25 through July, 1805

While Seaman was recovering, the countryside was changing. Leaving the grassy plains, the boats entered an area as dry as a desert. On each side of the river, the land rose into sandy cliffs. Sand blew into the explorers' faces, stinging their eyes and sticking to their skin.

In this remote area, the explorers caught their first glimpse of the shining mountains the Indians had described. Looking toward the west, they could see the distant Rockies gleaming white in the sunshine. Although the mountains were a beautiful sight, the men shivered. They knew those shining peaks were covered with snow! Somehow, the Corps of Discovery would have to cross those frozen peaks to reach the western sea.

The river twisted around endless curves, and the jagged cliffs slashed straight down into the water on both sides of the river. A strong downstream wind always blew. The men found they could not sail or paddle the boats against this wind and current, so they pulled the boats with ropes. They cut their feet on the rocky river bottom as they trudged through the water. Their ropes dried out and snapped, and the white pirogue was nearly lost once again, this time in the rocky water. As soon as the explorers solved one problem, another arose to slow their progress.

As they continued west, the explorers recognized the area the Indians called the White Cliffs. Sandstone cliffs towered above them, two hundred feet and higher. Their weathered surfaces were chipped and pitted; they looked like the windowed walls of ancient ruins. Although the men were very tired, they marveled at this stark scenery. It was as different from the green, rolling landscape of the eastern United States as any place they could imagine.

During the night of May 29, when everyone was sound asleep except one night guard, a buffalo accidentally blundered into camp. The great hulk of a bull swam across the river and climbed right over the white pirogue, which was beached on the riverbank with both captains sleeping in it. Luckily, the massive animal, which weighed a ton or more, did not fall on the boat. The captains were not even roused by the sounds of its hooves crunching on the stony beach.

Four campfires were burning in the nearby camp, and the flickering blazes confused the bull. It snorted, terrified. Its sides twitched, and it stamped its hooves on the rocky ground. In a frantic search for an escape from this strange place, it began to run, swerving wildly from side to side.

Seaman was dozing beside the guard by one of the campfires. Hearing the noise, he began to bark. In the darkness, the guard called out, but the man could not figure out what was causing the commotion. Some of the explorers sat up, dazed with sleep. Others rolled over and reached for their firearms.

The bull's panic increased as the darkened shapes on the ground began to move. It stampeded through the camp, trampling on a rifle and a gun. Its hooves came within inches of sleeping men's heads. Desperate to escape, it lowered its head and charged toward the tent where the sergeants, as well as Charbonneau, Sacagawea, and the baby, slept.

Seaman dashed through the camp, barking ferociously. The buffalo was only a few yards away from ramming into the tent when Seaman caught up with it. Growling and snapping at the bull's heels, Seaman turned the buffalo away from the tent and drove it out of camp.

When Seaman returned to camp, everyone was awake. Men were checking the sleeping rolls to be sure nobody had been trampled. Miraculously, not a single person had been injured, and only a few firearms had been damaged!

"Seaman, I don't know what we would do without you!" Shannon exclaimed, spreading out his arms to hug the dog.

Seaman jumped up, put his front paws on Shannon's chest, and licked the young man's face. Then he trotted around the camp. Inside the tent, the dog spotted Charbonneau, who was muttering sleepily. The sergeants patted Seaman gratefully, delighted by their good fortune. Sacagawea's baby had not even awakened.

Lewis called Seaman to his side and stroked his head. "Thank God nobody was trampled by that beast!" he said. "You saved our lives tonight, Seaman!"

For the next few weeks, Seaman's barking often woke the explorers during the night. In the mornings, the men sometimes discovered buffalo herds near the outskirts of camp. Occasionally they spotted signs of grizzly. No matter how often the barking woke them up, none of the explorers ever complained. Seaman had become the camp's guard.

The explorers proceeded on until they reached a fork in the river. Here the men stopped, puzzled. The river from the north was muddy—the river from the south was clear. Which waterway was the Missouri River? The men made camp and discussed the matter. The captains thought the clear river from the south was the Missouri, and the river coming down from the north was only a tributary. Everyone else disagreed, thinking the muddy river must be the Missouri. Finally, the captains decided to take scouting parties to explore both rivers.

As soon as Lewis and his six scouts packed their gear for the trip, he called Seaman. He knelt and stroked the dog's chest, then he walked over to Sacagawea with the dog by his side.

"Sit, Seaman," Lewis said.

Seaman sat obediently. He cocked his head and looked at Lewis.

"That's right, Seaman! Stay," Lewis said firmly. He told Sacagawea, "Be sure Seaman stays in camp with you for a few hours."

Sacagawea looked puzzled. "The dog's leg is better," she said. "He is strong now."

"Yes, he's strong enough to run with my scouting party. But Seaman is the best night guard we have," Lewis explained. "Remember the night the buffalo stampeded through camp? Most of our people and all of our supplies will be here in camp. The dog should stay to keep you safe."

Sacagawea nodded and smiled. She laid her hand on Seaman's head.

Clark's scouting party returned on June 6, and Lewis's party returned on the eighth. The captains were convinced the northern river was a tributary running out of the northern prairie, and not the Missouri River, which was believed to flow out of the Rocky Mountains. But the others still thought the Missouri was the northern river. The captains decided to send out another scouting party to find a major landmark—the Missouri's gigantic waterfalls—which the Indians at Fort Mandan had described. As soon as they found those falls, they would know they were on the right river.

The plan was for Lewis to lead the scouting party to find the waterfalls. Once he found Great Falls, Lewis would be in charge of deciding the best land route around it. Since the boats could not travel up the waterfalls, the men would have to portage, carrying all their boats and supplies overland.

Again, Lewis insisted on leaving Seaman in camp as a guard.

"Meriwether," Clark declared, "I fear you're going to break your dog's heart! When my scouting party arrived back in camp, Seaman was moping around, looking miserable."

Lewis called Seaman to his side and knelt to gaze into the dog's deep brown eyes. "Seaman," Lewis said, "your job is to guard our camp. It's a very important job. Your senses are so keen that you're the best guard we have."

Seaman's tail swished back and forth along the ground. He nuzzled Lewis's hand.

Lewis turned to Clark. "William, I'd love to take Seaman with me. But I promised President Jefferson I'd give my life, if necessary, to make this expedition a success. And I meant it. The camp is safer when Seaman is here. He needs to stay."

So it was decided. On June 11, Lewis took four men to explore the southern river, and Seaman remained with Clark. In camp, the men began to prepare for the portage around Great Falls. To lighten their load, they divided their supplies—some to be taken on the trip west, and the rest to be stored in a cache. The men dug a large hole to make the cache. They left some tightly sealed kegs of dried food and a keg of salt in the hole. They also left heavy tools, like the blacksmith bellows, some of the guns, and gunpowder. Since the pirogues were too big and awkward for travel on the smaller headwaters of the Missouri, the men left one of them on top of the cache. They planned to leave the second pirogue in another cache further upriver. They threw dirt and branches and leaves on the pile, and concealed it so neither animals nor Indians would find the supplies. The men planned to pick up the pirogues and the supplies on their return trip.

Lewis's scouting party found the Great Falls of the Missouri on June 13. It was even more spectacular than the Indians had described. In his journal, Lewis called it "the grandest sight I ever beheld." As soon as he located this landmark, Lewis knew that he and Clark had been correct. The southern river, the clear river, was the Missouri.

Unfortunately, Great Falls was not a single waterfall. Instead, it was five separate, mighty waterfalls with rapids between them. This was very bad news, because it meant the men would have to carry the boats and supplies much farther than they expected—nearly twenty miles over rough ground!

As Lewis returned to camp, Seaman ran to meet him. He barked excitedly. Lewis put out his hand to stroke the dog, but Seaman turned and dashed away, leading the men toward camp. He stopped several yards down the trail and barked again. His barks were short, loud, and urgent.

Lewis was at first puzzled by Seaman's behavior. Suddenly, he understood. "Something's wrong!" he shouted to the men in his scouting party. They began to run, following Seaman toward camp.

Clark greeted the party with the bad news: "It's Sacagawea," he explained, a worried look on his face. "She took ill after you left. It seems to be her stomach. I've tried everything I could think of, but she doesn't seem any better."

Striding quickly to the tent with Seaman by his side, Lewis was alarmed by what he found: Sacagawea was very weak, with a high fever and strained breathing. She said she had awful pains in her abdomen. Seaman licked the young woman's face, nuzzling her gently. She smiled faintly, and reached a weak hand up to pat the dog's chest.

As he examined the Indian woman, Lewis recalled Sergeant Floyd, who had died with a stomach complaint in the early months of their journey. None of their remedies had saved the young sergeant, and all of the men were greatly saddened by his death. Now the captain prayed for the skill to save this young Indian mother.

Since he did not know the cause of her illness, Lewis treated Sacagawea by restricting her diet to mineral water from a nearby spring. To relieve the pain, he laid warm, moist cloths on her abdomen and gave her medicines that he had brought on the journey. He watched her carefully, responding to each of her symptoms. He had tried a similar approach on Sergeant Floyd, but this time, to everybody's relief, Lewis's doctoring seemed to help.

While Sacagawea slowly grew stronger, the men took turns caring for her son. By now Jean-Baptiste was a healthy, fat, four-month-old. His little round face and his funny gurgling sounds enchanted everybody in the Corps. York moistened the parched corn they had brought from Fort Mandan to make mush for him to eat. The men played peekaboo with him while York fed him with a spoon. If the baby squirmed, Seaman darted to his side and licked his chubby toes.

Whenever he had a minute, Captain Clark picked the baby up and bounced him gently on his knee. If the baby cried, Clark held him close against his shoulder while he hummed tunes from his own nursery days. The baby usually had such a serious expression on his face that Clark nicknamed him "Pomp." Soon all the explorers called him Pomp.

During Sacagawea's illness, the men got ready for the portage. Fortunately, after the expedition had left the White Cliffs, they entered grassy countryside again. Small trees grew along the banks of the river, and the men cut them down for wood to make into wagons. They sawed cross sections from the trunk of a cottonwood tree to get large wooden circles that could be used as wheels. Then they loaded supplies onto their makeshift wagons. They were going to have to push, pull, or carry the wagons nearly twenty miles around the falls to reach a place where the river's waters were calm enough for boats again. They also made a second cache of supplies and left the white pirogue in it.

One evening in camp, Lewis called Seaman. Lewis was holding leather saddlebags, two pouches held together by straps and buckles. "Stand, boy. Stay." Lewis had sewn an extra strap between the pouches so the saddlebags could be worn like a harness, with one strap over Seaman's back, another that buckled around his belly, and a third strap that ran across his chest. "Let's see if you'll put up with these saddlebags, Seaman. The men can use all the help they can get with the portage."

Lewis let Seaman sniff the leather saddlebags. Then he slipped the dog's head through the straps. Lewis knelt and pulled the chest strap into place. The pouches hung against Seaman's sides from the strap over his back. Lewis buckled the belly strap loosely around Seaman's middle. Seaman jerked his head around and chewed the belly strap, trying to yank it off.

"No, Seaman," Lewis said firmly. "Stand still."

Seaman looked at Lewis. He whined and wagged his tail. Lewis took up some of the slack in the belly strap, then he stuffed a few pieces of clothing in the pouches to give them a little weight. He backed up and called, "Come, Seaman."

Seaman took a step forward, then hesitated. He looked over his shoulder at the saddlebags.

"That's a good boy, Seaman," Lewis said encouragingly. "Come."

Seaman took a few more steps, glancing back at the pouches on either side of him. He finally reached Lewis and started to sit, but he sprang up when he felt the saddlebags touch his thighs. He studied Lewis's face, trying to figure out how to play this new game.

"It's all right, fellow!" Lewis said and stroked Seaman's head and back. He put a hand on Seaman's rump and sat him down. "That's not so bad, is it?" Lewis placed a small metal tool in each of the pouches. Then he walked a few yards away and again told Seaman to come.

The dog jumped up and trotted over. The saddlebags jiggled from side to side as he moved. This time Seaman reached Lewis and sat with no hesitation.

Lewis knelt down and stroked Seaman. "What a smart boy you are!"

Seaman licked Lewis's face.

"You're going to help us carries supplies on the portage, Seaman."

the prickly pears were extreemly troublesome to us sticking our feet....
—JOURNAL OF CAPTAIN MERIWETHER LEWIS, June 22, 1805

Lewis loaded up the saddlebags and let Seaman practice carrying them several times. As soon as Seaman got used to the feel of the saddlebags against his fur, he trotted along cheerfully. He hardly noticed the weight of the pouches.

Each time they practiced, Lewis walked farther away before telling Seaman to come. Finally, Lewis led Seaman to the edge of a small stand of trees. He told Seaman to stay and walked through trees and brush. Then he called, "Come, Seaman."

Seaman sprang forward to follow Lewis. The bulky saddlebags brushed against some branches, and Seaman stopped, puzzled. He looked back at the pouches, then started walking again. Suddenly, Seaman could not move. He had followed Lewis into a narrow space between two trees, but the saddlebags made him too wide to fit through. Seaman barked once, then whined.

Lewis chuckled. "You've got to leave more room for yourself when you're carrying loaded saddlebags, Seaman." He started back to help the dog.

Seaman backed up and darted around the trees, running to Lewis.

Lewis smiled. "Now you've got it figured out. Smart boy!" He tapped his chest, and Seaman bounded to him and jumped up,

resting his paws lightly on Lewis's chest. Lewis threw his arms around the dog, letting Seaman lick his face. "Wait till the men see you carrying these saddlebags, Seaman!"

The next morning, Lewis packed up the saddlebags and buckled them around Seaman. When Seaman joined the men, his tail was wagging proudly.

Colter was the first to notice. "Seaman, you're carrying a backpack!" he said, smiling.

Seaman panted, his mouth wide open as if he were grinning, and padded over to Colter, who smoothed the velvety fur on top of the dog's head.

The other men called Seaman over to stroke him or to give him chunks of dried meat. Of all the explorers, Seaman was the only one who seemed to be looking forward to the portage.

The portage was exhausting. Hour after hour, day after day, the explorers trudged across the rough ground. Sweat poured off their foreheads and pasted their clothes to their backs. The wagons got stuck and had to be yanked out of holes. Wheels fell off, axles broke. Countless times each day, the men had to stop to repair the crude wagons and reload their supplies.

Seaman walked alongside the men and their wagons, his saddlebags stuffed with supplies. The weight didn't bother him at all, but he was bothered by the prickly pear cactus growing all over the uneven ground. The plant's long, stiff spines stuck in the pads of his paws. Seaman chewed and pulled out the larger spines, but his pads became covered with finer spines that stung whenever he walked. Sometimes the pain made him yelp.

The cactus spines pierced the soles of the men's leather moccasins and cut their feet. The men sewed double layers of leather on the bottoms of their moccasins, but still their footwear would last only two days. Their feet became sore and bloody.

The sight of Seaman working beside them encouraged the weary men. As soon as they reached the river and the men unloaded Seaman's bags, he leaped into the water. The cool water soothed his sore paws. Some of the men followed his example and jumped in, soaking their tired muscles for a few minutes before walking back to camp to load up more supplies.

At last the painful portage was finished. But the explorers could not get back in the boats yet. Since they had left the pirogues behind in the caches, they needed to make more canoes to carry everyone. So the men searched for large trees, cut them down, and hollowed out the insides to make dugout canoes. It took a month for the explorers to portage their supplies and make new canoes, and in that month they traveled only about twenty miles up the river.

On July 15, the Corps of Discovery was finally ready to continue. The explorers had eight sturdy canoes—two large and six smaller. Their supplies had been trimmed down to essentials. The men's sore feet were healing. Sacagawea was healthy again, and little Pomp was safely strapped to the board on her back. New fur covered the scar where Seaman's beaver wound had been.

Now the explorers turned their thoughts to the shining mountains. All they had to do was cross the Rockies, they thought. Then they would race downstream to the sea!

CHAPTER NINE

SEARCHING FOR THE SHOSHONE

Mid-July through August 31, 1805

Seaman splashed into the cold, clear water to escape the suffocating summer heat. He plunged his head under the river's surface to rid his eyes of the pesky gnats. But as soon as he scrambled out of the water, the sun beat down on his back again, and the gnats swarmed all over his face.

The Missouri River no longer resembled its nickname, "Old Muddy." Now it was a swift mountain stream tumbling over rocks and rushing around cliffs. As the men fought against its current, sweat slid down their necks. Sometimes the current was so strong they couldn't paddle or pole against it, so they had to pull the canoes with ropes for hours. All the while, the sun baked their shoulders and the chilly water numbed their legs. Mosquitoes buzzed around their ears.

As the explorers followed the river toward its source, they were heading south. To their right, the Rocky Mountains stood like a wall between them and the western sea. The men shuddered when they looked at these pointed peaks, which seemed to pierce the very heavens. Unlike the tree-covered, rounded slopes of the Appalachian range, the Rockies were jagged and steep, with snowy tops. Secretly, each man wondered whether the expedition would be able to cross such rugged mountains.

The captains had already made a plan for the crossing. They knew that the Shoshone Indians, Sacagawea's people, lived on the eastern side of the Rockies. The Shoshones had plenty of horses. With Sacagawea's help as a translator, Lewis and Clark planned to trade for enough horses to carry the expedition's supplies. The captains hoped the Shoshones might also be willing to supply an Indian guide to show them the way through the steep mountains.

On July 19, Captain Lewis led the expedition up the river while Captain Clark took a small party of men overland to search for the Shoshones. On the river, the canoes entered a canyon where rocky walls rose more than a thousand feet. The water was too deep for the men to stand in it. They crossed through dark shadows cast by towering cliffs. The place was so remarkable that Lewis struggled for words to describe it. He finally named it "the Gates of the Rocky Mountains."

As the canoes emerged from the canyon, Seaman woofed. His keen nose had picked up the smell of smoke. He rushed from one end of the canoe to the other, tensed for danger. The dugout canoe rocked with his movements.

Lewis stood and scanned the sky. He spotted a thick column of smoke about seven miles away. A large area of the prairie seemed to be burning. Lewis groaned.

"What's wrong, Captain?" asked George Shannon.

"That fire must have been deliberately set." Lewis said.

"You think Captain Clark is signalling to us?"

Lewis shook his head sadly. "I doubt it. Clark wouldn't have set the prairie on fire."

"So, Indians must have set the fire," Shannon said cheerfully. "Guess we'll be meeting up with a band of Shoshones today or tomorrow."

Lewis's face was grim. His eyes met Sacagawea's, and she nodded sadly, confirming his suspicions. "It's not going to be easy to meet up with the Shoshones now. More than likely, this fire was set by Indian scouts to warn their people of strangers in the area." Lewis frowned. "The scouts must have decided we're a war party. So they set a big, noticeable fire to tell their band to keep out of sight."

"Captain, if the Shoshones don't let us get near them, what will we do?" Shannon asked. "Without horses, how will we be able to get across the mountains before winter sets in?"

Lewis did not answer, and they sat in silence for several minutes. Soon, Pomp awoke with a small whimper, and Sacagawea slid his cradleboard off her shoulders. Seaman nuzzled Pomp's cheeks, bringing a smile to the baby's face. Sacagawea began to nurse her baby, and she sang a quiet, soothing song. As they listened to the song, Seaman edged closer to Lewis. His tail thumped gently, and Lewis's face began to relax. So far, the captain reflected, the Corps had found a way to overcome every challenge. They would find a way to cross the Rockies. And if they didn't? Well, Lewis, for one, was willing to die trying!

A few days later, on July 22, Sacagawea sat up and looked carefully at the land beside the river. "I have been here before—when I was a girl," she told Lewis. She spoke quietly, but with conviction.

Lewis stared at her. "You recognize this place?" he asked. "Are you sure?"

Sacagawea smiled. "Yes, I know this place," she said confidently. "In summer, my people sometimes camped along the banks of this river. Soon we will reach Three Forks, where three rivers join together to form the Missouri River."

Lewis's mind was racing. If Sacagawea's people came here every summer, then surely the Shoshone were somewhere nearby. The explorers ought to be able to find them.

Late that afternoon, Seaman began to bark, his tail wagging excitedly. The men steadied the canoe and searched the bank of the river. It was Captain Clark and his scouting party! The boats pulled close to shore, and Lewis jumped out, with Seaman splashing beside him.

"William, we are nearing the headwaters of the Missouri!" Lewis blurted out. "Sacagawea recognized this stretch of the river. She says her people camp here in summer. Have you seen any signs of the—"

Suddenly Lewis stopped speaking. Seaman was sniffing Clark's bare feet. They were a bloody mess!

"What happened to your feet?" Lewis cried in alarm.

"Prickly pear!" Clark replied with disgust. "That cursed cactus grows so thick around here, we couldn't avoid it. It ripped the soles of our moccasins to shreds."

Lewis knelt to examine the soles of Clark's feet. "Seems it also ripped the soles of your feet to shreds!"

The overland party had cuts and blisters covering every inch of their feet. Lewis treated the cuts and opened the blisters so they would drain. He insisted the men stay off their feet for a day to let them heal. But the overland party had worse news than prickled feet. They had not succeeded in finding the Shoshones. And without Shoshone horses, the captains had no idea how to get across the mountains.

Clark was determined to try again, despite his torn feet, and he set out the next day with three men. Lewis proceeded up the river with the rest of the Corps.

River travel became even harder. The current was swifter, the water was icier, but the sun remained every bit as hot. Walking along the riverbank was just as bad as boat duty. In Lewis's journal, he complained the expedition was bothered by a "trio of pests"—mosquitoes, eye gnats, and prickly pears. The men became so weary that Lewis tried to encourage them by adding his own muscle to the group's efforts: The captain himself took turns poling one of the canoes!

As soon as travel conditions seemed as bad as they could get, they got worse. The explorers discovered needlegrass, a plant with sharp seeds that poked right through leather and stuck in their skin. The seeds had to be picked off one by one. Poor Seaman suffered mightily from this new pest. Lewis wrote that his dog was "constantly binting and scratching himself as if in a rack of pain."

"Maybe this river doesn't have an end," York said one evening. He was picking needlegrass seeds out of the legs of his buckskin pants. "Maybe it just twists around like a big old knot and we'll go round and round on it, retracing our own steps."

Colter grinned. "It has to have an end, York. Every river has an end. We just haven't found it yet."

Seaman gnawed at his back legs, trying to pull out needlegrass seeds. Colter sat down on the ground next to him. "Take it easy, Seaman. You're going to chew holes in your skin."

Colter began to pick the seeds out of the dog's fur, and Seaman stretched out on his side, panting. After a few minutes, Colter gently stroked the dog's fur. "That's all I can do, Seaman. It's so dark I can't see the seeds anymore."

"Maybe this here river does have an end," York continued, "but you think we're ever going to find it? Seems to me the days are getting shorter. I used to finish cooking supper before it got dark. Now I can hardly gather the kindling before dark."

Colter stared at the black river. "It does get dark sooner every day, York. Winter always comes early in the high country."

"Captain Clark says we can't cross the mountains in winter. You reckon we'll make winter camp out here?"

"I don't think there's enough game out here to last the winter," Colter said. "We haven't seen a herd of buffalo in days. If we don't get across the Rockies soon, I think the expedition will have to turn back."

The river began to curve toward the southeast, which worried Lewis. That meant they were traveling in a direction exactly opposite their goal. The men's spirits sank as low as the river's chilly bottom. Not even Seaman, splashing merrily through the water, could bring a smile to Lewis's face. Unless their luck changed—and changed quickly—the Lewis and Clark expedition seemed to be doomed.

On July 27, the river came into a wide valley. A second river rushed at the men, and a little ways upstream a third river rushed downstream to join the other waterways. At last, they had reached the spot described by the Indians at Fort Mandan and by Sacagawea—Three Forks!

Lewis ordered the men to pull the canoes onto the banks. He whistled for Seaman, and they climbed a nearby hill. Below them were the two valleys. To the south and east, they could see the two rivers flowing through one of the valleys, and from the southwest came the third river flowing through the second valley. The waters from all three rivers merged into the Missouri.

Lewis sat on the ground and patted his leg for Seaman to sit beside him. As he stroked Seaman's fur, his mood began to lift. The green valleys striped with rivers lay below them. Around them, snowcapped mountains formed a jagged border against the sky. No other American citizen had ever seen this beautiful place, Lewis thought. The Corps of Discovery had come so far! He wanted to preserve this sight—this moment—in his mind. Even if they didn't reach the Pacific Ocean, he told himself, the explorers had accomplished so much.

The Corps made camp at Three Forks. That afternoon, Clark and his overland party tramped in wearily. Clark was feeling sick, with a fever and muscle aches. Even worse, he reported that his party had not spotted a single Shoshone.

The explorers stayed at Three Forks for the next two days while Clark recovered. There was plenty to do. The men tanned hides to make clothes and moccasins. Colter took Seaman out hunting. Although there were no buffalo, deer were still plentiful, and Colter brought back several bucks. York and Charbonneau prepared hearty meals for the tired travelers.

As they sat around the evening fire, Cruzatte played his fiddle and Shannon sang a silly song to amuse baby Pomp. Seaman settled down near the baby, rested his head on his front paws, and dozed. When Sacagawea began to speak, Seaman lifted his head and cocked his ears. All of the explorers stopped to listen, for Sacagawea ordinarily spoke very little.

"This is the place, five summers ago, where I last saw my family." Her steady voice told the story of the Hidatsa raiding party that came upon her Shoshone camp. "We ran for three miles and hid ourselves in the woods.

"But the Hidatsa braves chased us. When they found us, they killed four of our men and four of our women. And they killed many of our young boys. Most of us became their prisoners. They took us far away from this place. Far down the Missouri River, the same river we have just traveled up so many miles. They took us to their villages, near Fort Mandan."

George Shannon looked at Sacagawea's eyes, bright in the firelight. "How old were you when you were taken prisoner?" he asked.

"I had seen twelve summers," she said simply.

Although her words were heartbreaking, Sacagawea spoke without any display of her feelings. She did not weep or complain. This was her story, and she accepted it as the grass accepts the sun and the sky accepts the thunder.

Nobody spoke. After a few minutes, Cruzatte played a slow, lonely song on his fiddle.

When the men of the Corps were living at Fort Mandan, the last landmark the Indians could describe to them was Three Forks. Now that the expedition had reached Three Forks, the captains were on their own. Nobody had given them any advice about which way to continue traveling west. They didn't know which of the three forks to follow, so they chose the river that curved to the west, since that was the direction of the Pacific Ocean. They named it the Jefferson River in honor of the president.

While Clark led the canoes up the river, Lewis led short scouting parties overland to search for Shoshone Indians. He left

Seaman with the canoes, because the Shoshones might be scared off by the sight of such a big dog. But Lewis's luck was no better than Clark's had been.

On August 8, Sacagawea recognized another landmark: a rise her people called the "Beaver's Head." She said this was near a place where the Shoshone lived during the summer months.

Now this was encouraging news! Lewis took two men and set out to locate the Indians, leaving Seaman with Clark and the others.

Canoe travel had become impossibly slow. The Jefferson River was more like a shallow stream than a river. There were frustrating delays when the canoes got stuck on boulders or tree roots. Seaman splashed along the icy, shallow water as the men strained against the ropes. The group came to the mouth of another stream, and Clark wasn't sure which waterway was the Jefferson River. Although they kept expecting to see Lewis or one of his scouts return with some news, days passed with no word.

On August 17, the men were dragging the canoes when Seaman barked and took off at a gallop. A few minutes later, he returned with one of Lewis's scouts and an Indian brave. The Indian was so thin his ribs stuck out. He wore a cloth around his waist, a baggy vest, and a brightly colored cloth headband.

Clark waved. He turned to Sacagawea and asked, "Is the brave one of your people?"

Sacagawea smiled and nodded. "He wears the clothing of my people."

"Captain Clark," called the scout, "Captain Lewis is in camp with the Shoshone chief. We saw the Indians' horse herd. They have about four hundred animals!"

Clark told the explorers to beach the boats. He ordered some men to guard the supplies and told the others to follow him. Taking Sacagawea, Charbonneau, and Seaman, he hurried ahead. As they rounded a bend, Seaman dashed up the bank, barking happily. In a minute, Clark saw Lewis waving to them, his face beaming. Seaman bounded to Lewis, wagging his tail.

Lewis threw his arms around Seaman, letting the dog cover his face with wet kisses. He buried his hands in Seaman's warm fur and gave a silent prayer of thanks. At last, the Corps of Discovery was together again! They had finally located the Shoshones, and the Indians had plenty of horses to trade!

The Indians crowded around, eager for a look at the newcomers. Clark ran up to Lewis and held him by his shoulders. "Meriwether, you did it! You found the Shoshones!"

"I am so glad to see you, William! We've been camped here for days, waiting." Lewis's words rushed out. "When you didn't come, the Indians started grumbling. They thought I was playing some sort of trick on them. I was afraid they would leave before you arrived with the trade goods."

Lewis stroked Seaman's head and told him to sit. "Stay, Seaman." Seaman responded immediately. He sat, his eyes searching Lewis's face. He did not move a muscle, except the tip of his tail, which wagged back and forth.

Then Lewis led Clark to the Shoshone chief, Cameahwait. The chief grasped Clark and gave him a full body hug, a traditional greeting among Shoshone men. Cameahwait decorated Clark's hair with shells to honor him. The Indians gathered around to watch, smiling at the explorers. These men were the first people the Shoshones had ever seen who were not Indians!

The greetings began, and the explorers found themselves smothered with hugs. Several of the Shoshones marvelled at Seaman. They made the sign for bear and seemed astonished that the big dog would sit so patiently. The Indians said the dog's intelligence was astonishing! The Indians also seemed amazed that a man could have black skin. They eagerly touched the bare skin on York's neck and arms when they hugged him.

Suddenly, a woman screamed! Everyone froze, startled. Seaman woofed and sprang to his feet. His eyes scanned the people's faces, searching for danger.

One of the Shoshone women clutched Sacagawea, and both began to cry out. The women recognized each other—they had been childhood friends! The two were in the same camping party when the Hidatsa raiders took Sacagawea prisoner. In fact, the woman had acquired her name, Jumping Fish, from the way she had leaped across the stream to escape from the Hidatsas!

The explorers watched, astonished, as quiet, calm Sacagawea screamed and danced around, weeping with joy. The two young women hugged, tears streaming down their cheeks. Then they laughed through their tears, grasping each others' shoulders to gaze in wonder into each others' faces. Words tumbled from their mouths.

After a few minutes, the women quieted down. Sacagawea slid Pomp off her back and showed him to her friend. Jumping Fish held the baby in her arms and drenched him with teary kisses.

Late that afternoon, after the greetings were finished, the captains held a meeting with Cameahwait and some of his braves. Sacagawea was the translator, and Seaman sat calmly by her side.

The men were deep into their talk when Sacagawea suddenly stopped translating. She leaned forward, her eyes fixed on Cameahwait. Puzzled, the captains stared at her.

Ignoring the awkward silence, Sacagawea called out a few words in Shoshone. She jumped up and ran to Chief Cameahwait. Then she threw her arms around him and held him.

Lewis looked at Charbonneau. "What's going on?" he asked.

"Sacagawea just recognized her brother!"

Astounded, the men stared. Sacagawea called the Shoshone chief by his childhood name. Cameahwait smoothed his sister's hair, looked into her eyes, and tenderly held her slender face in his large, weathered hands. Sacagawea unwound the blanket tied around her waist and threw it over their heads so she could weep with Cameahwait in private. Sobs shook her body as she held her

The Great Chief of this nation proved to be the brother of the Woman with us and is a man of Influence Sence &…Cincerity.

—JOURNAL OF CAPTAIN WILLIAM CLARK, August 17, 1805

brother, now a grown man and the leader of the people she had been torn from as a girl.

After a while, Sacagawea returned quietly to her seat in the circle. Seaman crept to her side. She laid a hand on the dog's broad back as if to steady herself. The men resumed their talk, and Sacagawea translated. Tears streamed down her cheeks, and several times her face crumpled. She had to pause and hold her hand in front of her eyes, struggling to compose herself. Finally, she nodded at the captains, and the meeting continued.

Cameahwait remained calm, as befitted the leader of his people. But his eyes looked lovingly on this young woman who had been a little girl when last they called each other brother and sister.

The Shoshone Indians helped the explorers carry their baggage over the first high pass in the Rockies. Seaman ran alongside the Indians and the explorers on the steep trail, wearing his saddlebags packed full of goods. Food was scarce, but the two groups shared what little they had. By August 26, the work was complete. That night, the explorers held a party in camp to thank the Indians. Cruzatte played his fiddle and the men danced. York danced a jig, and the Indians called out their appreciation for his nimble feet.

It was a merry evening, but the leaders of both groups were nervous. Early that morning, there had been frost. The Shoshones were eager to reach the buffalo hunting grounds on the Plains to lay in a store of meat for the winter. Without this food supply, their band would starve in the coming months. The explorers had to get enough horses to carry them aross the mountains before the snows came, or their group would also starve to death.

Over the next few days, horse trading occupied most of the leaders' time. Seaman sat near the captains as they haggled for horses. At first, bargaining was easy. The Indians were delighted to trade such a common item as a horse for novelties like cloth shirts or mirrors. But soon the Indians realized the explorers were desperate to acquire horses and would pay whatever they could. In just a few days, the price of Shoshone horses greatly increased. The explorers bargained away some of their dearest possessions—knives, guns, and ammunition. In the end, they got their horses, twenty-nine of them, but the animals did not come cheaply.

It was not the Shoshone custom to travel west toward the Pacific Ocean. But one older man in their band, Old Toby, had made this journey years ago. He knew the way through the mountains, and he agreed to guide the expedition.

Both the Indians and the explorers were keenly aware that winter was closing in. It was critical to be on their separate ways. For Sacagawea, this was a painful thought. She had been torn away from her family, friends, and homeland when she was only a girl of twelve. For so many years, she held no hope of seeing any of her people again. Miraculously, in the last two weeks, she had been reunited with both her brother and her childhood friend.

But she was a young mother herself, now, with her own husband and family. She had a job to do for the Corps of Discovery. Together with Charbonneau and the explorers, she turned toward the west and the unknown lands leading to the Pacific Ocean. How she yearned in her heart to be turning east with the people of her birth!

Sacagawea said her farewells to her people. As always, she accepted her future without complaint, as a stream accepts melting snow in spring and cooling rain in autumn.

Seaman stayed close to the horse that Sacagawea rode as the explorers waved good-bye to the Shoshones. He sensed that this trail was steeper for the young Indian woman than for the other explorers.

CHAPTER TEN

THE STARVING TIME

September, 1805

When the Corps of Discovery entered mountain country, Seaman was only one of many four-footed members of the expedition. A small herd of horses trudged along with the explorers. Some of the horses carried riders, others carried baggage. Seaman jogged comfortably along beside the horses' legs, his fur waving and the skin on his back rolling from side to side. The Shoshone horses were used to running with Indian dogs, and calm-natured Seaman did not frighten them.

Until now, the Missouri River had been a sort of map through the wilderness. But when the explorers entered the Rocky Mountains, there were no clear landmarks to follow. They blundered through dense patches of tangled bushes. Thorny branches snagged the men's buckskin clothing and scratched their faces. They struggled up rocky hillsides with slopes as steep as the roof of a house.

Sometimes loose stones shifted beneath the horses' feet, and they lost their footing. Whenever a horse stumbled, Seaman ran back and urged it on.

The explorers followed Old Toby, their Shoshone guide, into this rugged landscape. They accepted his directions and trusted his judgment completely. Even the captains were too preoccupied with the difficulty of traveling to worry about the route. Although the men had horses to carry the baggage and they had left behind the heavy canoes, the land was so rough that the expedition only covered about fifteen miles each day.

On September 3, rain and sleet made the rocky ground slippery. That night, there was a hard freeze. The hunters came in empty-handed, except for a few grouse. Reluctantly, the captains ordered the last of the salt pork to be distributed.

"And for the dog?" asked Charbonneau as he passed out supper. "Also a share of the pork?"

"Of course," Colter replied quickly. "He earns his share. Just like the rest of us."

Charbonneau looked at Captain Lewis, who nodded. Charbonneau cut off a hunk of the meat and tossed it to Seaman.

"Chew it slowly, Seaman," Colter said. "That's not much supper for a big fellow like you."

"That's right," York said, washing down some of his meat with a gulp of water. "And this is all the meat we got in the pantry!"

Shannon flopped down beside Seaman and grinned playfully. "You better listen to our advice, Seaman. If you 'wolf' down your supper, you'll have to sit and drool while everybody else is still chewing."

He ruffled Seaman's fur. "Of course, I didn't mean to insult you by comparing you to a wolf. Everybody knows wolves have no manners. And wolves, after all, are only distant cousins of the more noble dogs, such as you Newfoundlands!"

Shannon glared at Charbonneau. "Why, even among people," he said, "we all have relatives or acquaintances that we're not too proud of!"

Most of the men chuckled. Seaman paused from his supper and licked Shannon's nose. Shannon wrinkled up his face and made a big show of mopping off the dog's greasy kiss.

"Very funny, Monsieur Shannon," Charbonneau grumbled, his face red. "You make the jokes tonight, and all the men laugh at Charbonneau. But I think you will not be so funny tomorrow. This is the last of our pork, so I think I should be careful about who gets a share of meat.

"Today, our hunters were able to find only a few grouse," Charbonneau continued. "And grouse are such skinny birds—they have more feathers than meat!" He rolled his eyes in disgust. "So tonight you make fun of Charbonneau. Tomorrow you may not be so merry. We are in the middle of the mountains, and we do not know where our next meal will come from."

Fortunately, a band of about four hundred Indians crossed paths with the Corps the next day. They were on the way to meet their allies, the Shoshones, for the autumn buffalo hunt.

Old Toby introduced the Indian chiefs to the captains, who gave out a few medals and small gifts. Although the Indians' food supply was very limited, they shared their small stock of berries and roots. Before they parted company, the Indians also traded some of their horses, increasing the expedition's herd to more than forty animals.

That evening, Seaman received his share of dried berries and boiled roots, just like the other explorers. Luckily, York had saved the bones from the salt pork, and he boiled these with the roots to add flavor to the scanty meal. Seaman gobbled up his share of the meat-flavored roots and then licked up every dried berry in his little pile.

After he finished dishing out supper, York fished out the bones and laid them in front of Seaman. "There you go, big fellow," York said. "Maybe you can scrape out some of that marrow. Be more like the food a dog was meant to eat."

Seaman licked York's hand gratefully. He steadied the bones between his paws and gnawed until every crumb of marrow was gone. It wasn't much, but he went to bed no hungrier than the human explorers.

The last of the flour was used up by the sixth of September. Now the expedition's only food stock was a small amount of dried corn and some soup mix. The captains were worried, but Old Toby said they were nearing a valley where there was game to hunt.

Travel became easier when the explorers entered the Bitterroot Valley. The hunters brought in game. The expedition was able to speed up its pace and cover more than twenty miles a day.

After three days of travel through the valley, Old Toby sat beside Captain Lewis in front of the evening campfire. Seaman watched the Indian's wrinkled face and leathery hands. Old Toby spoke in signs, showing Lewis steep mountains by drawing in the air with his index finger. His expression was very serious as he warned Lewis about the route ahead. Sacagawea sat nearby, nursing Pomp. She listened carefully as Old Toby spoke and helped to translate some of his words so Lewis could understand them.

The expedition was about to leave the valley, Old Toby explained. The route would now take them west, following Lolo Creek into the high mountains.

Lewis nodded. This was the last camp before the explorers faced the most strenuous portion of the route. Old Toby said they should stock up on as much game as the hunters could find. The explorers would also need to gather their courage for the ordeal that lay ahead. The captains named this last camp in the valley "Travelers' Rest."

The next morning, September 10, all the hunters went out. John Colter whistled for Seaman, his favorite hunting companion. The pair ranged for miles in search of game. Suddenly, Seaman stood still, sniffing, and whined. Colter quickly dismounted, concealing himself and his horse in the shadows and signalling Seaman to join him.

Three Indians were coming toward them. Colter touched Seaman's nose with the palm of his hand to tell him to sit quietly. He studied the braves, trying to determine whether they were from a friendly tribe. Finally, Colter snapped a twig to announce his presence. Then he stepped out of the shadows with Seaman by his side.

Using signs, Colter invited the three Indians to follow him back to camp.

The Indians were from the Nez Perce, a tribe that lived west of the Rockies. They drew pictures on the ground to show they had recently left their village. The braves had just crossed the mountains and were heading east. According to them, it was only a journey of "five sleeps" across the mountains.

How the explorers rejoiced! In less than a week, they would be across the mountains. Surely, the Corps of Discovery could survive such a short trip, no matter how challenging the conditions!

"The hunters killed four deer today, William!" Lewis exclaimed happily as they sat around the campfire that evening. "And they brought back a beaver and three grouse, too. Even if we can't find any game in the mountains, we ought to be able to manage five days travel on these provisions. Not to mention what's left of our soup mix."

Clark added a note of caution. "The Indians seem to be able to travel faster than our men, Meriwether. Those braves say it's a five-day journey, but it may take us longer."

The next day, September 11, the explorers began climbing out of Bitterroot Valley. On the thirteenth, they passed a spring that bubbled out of the ground. Mists of steam rose from the water. Seaman reached the spring first. As soon as his paws touched the moist ground, he yelped and jumped backward, puzzled. The spring's waters were boiling hot!

York grabbed a pot to collect some of the hot water. He let it cool briefly, then he stripped off his shirt, splashing his face and chest with warm water. Grinning, he invited the others to join him. "This is the best bath I've had in months!" he declared.

They proceeded on, crossing Lolo Pass with surprising ease.

In the afternoon, Clark rode up to Lewis. "Seems the information we got from those Nez Perce Indians is right on target, Meriwether. We're making marvelous progress. This route is level, open, and firm." Delight sparkled in Clark's eyes. "We should be out of this high country in four days."

Lewis beamed, and his mind raced along the route ahead. "And then we'll find the Columbia River and glide downstream to the western sea!"

On September 14, it rained and hailed. The men's clothes got soaked, and the captains stopped smiling. Seaman shook water off his sopping coat every few minutes. Then the temperature dropped and the miserable rain froze. The ground became slippery with ice. To make bad matters worse, it started to snow. Old Toby got confused and led the expedition down the wrong ridge. The hunters came back cold and wet, with no game. That evening, the weary explorers had to kill a colt for supper.

Old Toby figured out his mistake the next day. But getting back to the trail was very difficult. Fallen trees were scattered all over the steep ground. The horses kept slipping. One horse rolled forty yards down a mountain until it slammed into a tree. Luckily, the horse survived the tumble without any injuries. But it had been carrying Captain Clark's writing desk, which was shattered.

The hunters again returned empty-handed except for two small grouse. York heated snow to make water, added the grouse and what was left of the colt, and handed out a thin meat soup for the evening meal. Again, he gave Seaman the bones to gnaw. Everybody went to sleep cold, hungry, and discouraged.

The snow began to fall three hours before dawn on September 16. When the explorers awoke, they found icy white powder on their faces, hair, and sleeping rolls. The snow continued all day, blanketing the ground in seven inches of slippery, white powder. Snow collected in fluffy little heaps on the branches of trees. As the men brushed against the branches, clumps of snow fell on their heads and melted. Icy water slithered down the necks of their shirts.

Seaman shook off the snow, but his outer coat got soaked anyway. Snow clumped between the pads of his paws, and he kept stopping to chew out the painful, icy balls.

That night, Clark complained in his journal: "I have been wet and as cold in every part as I ever was in my life." Cold, exhausted, and hungry, the men killed a second colt for supper.

The explorers had so little food they felt hungry all the time, but they were eating enough to keep themselves alive. Their horses, on the other hand, were starving; all of the grasses were dead or buried deep under snow. On the morning of September 17, the explorers awoke to Seaman barking. The whole herd of horses was missing. During the night, the animals had strayed all over the countryside in a desperate search for food.

The men began rounding up the animals at first light. It took hours. Seaman herded some of the strays by nipping at their heels to drive them back to camp. By the time the horses were collected and packed, much of the daylight had been wasted. Everybody was frustrated. The weather warmed up, but that only made traveling more uncomfortable. The snow melted into icy water and soaked through their moccasins.

That night, the explorers had to kill a third colt for supper. That was the last colt in their herd.

After the evening meal, Lewis checked the remaining supplies. Then he huddled with Clark, and the captains talked quietly. Seaman padded over to Lewis and sat close to him, gently nuzzling his master's hand.

"I fear we are reaching a breaking point," Lewis said, his tone gloomy and his eyes downcast.

"What is our stock?" Clark asked.

"I counted a few cannisters of dried soup mix, a bit of bear oil, and twenty pounds of candles. Hardly enough to sustain the needs of more than thirty people," Lewis replied.

Clark nodded. "Of course, we have our rifles and plenty of ammunition."

Lewis frowned. "The guns are little use in this country, where there is scarcely an animal to be found. When we hunted on the plains, the land yielded a feast. But up here, we're fortunate to find a few small grouse, some squirrels, or a couple of jays. In these mountains, the land yields famine."

"And the men are exhausted," Clark agreed sadly. "I find myself growing weak and light-headed for want of food."

The captains sat still, each deep in his own thoughts. The only movement was Lewis's hand rhythmically stroking Seaman's fur. Small comfort, perhaps. But in the absence of any other, the touch provided some relief from the heavy thoughts that weighed down the captains' minds.

"Perhaps we should kill one of the packhorses as food," suggested Clark.

Lewis shook his head. "No. That would mean abandoning some of our baggage. We don't know how far we must travel to reach the western sea, William. We already left everything we could spare in our last cache. What remains is essential."

Clark nodded and frowned. "It's five days travel back to the Bitterroot River, Meriwether. I don't think we have the strength to make it," he stated flatly.

"I'm not suggesting that we turn back!" Lewis spoke in a shocked voice. His face became a stone mask of determination. "Unthinkable! I would prefer to die than to quit."

"Agreed," Clark said simply. He looked around the camp. "But there are other lives to consider here, Meriwether. Not to mention information—a wealth of information. Our field notes and journals. The specimens for the scientists back East."

The captains' eyes met. "We must divide our force," Lewis said in a grim voice. "We must send a smaller group to hurry ahead to the level country to hunt. The advance group will send food back for the rest of our party."

Clark winced. "I dislike dividing the Corps, Meriwether. Especially now—when our very survival is at stake."

They were quiet for a minute, staring at the fire. Then Clark met Lewis's eyes. "But I agree. It's our best chance."

They decided Clark would take six of the best hunters as the advance group. Lewis would remain with the main party, which included Seaman, Old Toby, Charbonneau's family, most of the men, and all of the packhorses. Clark's group set out at dawn on September 18.

As soon as Lewis's group packed the horses, they proceeded on. On September 19, Lewis's group reached a narrow path beside a steep cliff. As they carefully made their way along the ledge, the men tried to avoid looking down at the three-hundred-foot drop beside them. All day long, the horses stumbled over the uneven ground, keeping as far as possible from the edge of the cliff. Each time a stone loosened and fell, Lewis gritted his teeth and prayed nobody would fall off the path. Their luck held. Although they sometimes slipped, the men and the horses were able to regain their shaky footing.

At dusk, their luck took a plunge: One of the packhorses started to slide and couldn't recover its foothold. Seaman barked to alert the men.

Several of the men dismounted and edged toward the horse in trouble. But they were unable to reach the animal. They watched helplessly as the horse rolled down and down. It landed with a great splash in the creek at the bottom of the cliff. The men scrambled down the slope to save what they could. Quickly, they untied the horse's load. Then they watched, amazed, as the animal rose shakily to its feet. The men shouldered the horse's load and led the trembling but unhurt animal back up the steep path.

The next morning, it was a silent group that plodded behind Old Toby. The hardships of the journey—the constant cramp of hunger, the extreme physical exertion, the fear of death in these mountains—were straining the explorers to the limits of their endurance.

Suddenly, Seaman pushed his nose into the air and sniffed deeply. He dashed ahead of the group, then returned and pranced excitedly around the legs of Lewis's horse, barking. Lewis hurried ahead, curious about what Seaman had discovered. There, he found a most welcome sight—a big bundle of fresh meat had been tied to an overhanging branch! Clark's advance group had killed a wild horse and left some of the meat for Lewis's party!

A twig was sticking out of the bundle, with a note on the end of it. Lewis leaped off his horse and grabbed the note. It told him that Clark's hunters were moving swiftly toward level ground. As soon as they were out of the mountains, they would begin hunting. Lewis shut his eyes and whispered, "Thank you, Lord."

The group immediately started a fire to prepare the food. Oh, the smell of the roasting meat! The explorer's mouths watered. Two long threads of drool dangled from Seaman's jaws.

The food lifted the group's spirits even before it filled their bellies. Seaman darted around the camp, retrieving a stick tossed by Shannon. York made a lightning-quick grab at the stick when Seaman ran past him and teased the dog into a tug of war. But the supper pot was about to boil over, so York gave up and let Seaman have the stick.

Seaman played with Shannon until supper was served. He wolfed down his share, but nobody objected. The men were eating just as hungrily as Seaman. His hunger eased for the first time in days, Seaman padded over to John Colter. He waited patiently while Colter finished eating. As soon as Colter licked up the last drop of his supper, Seaman rolled over onto his back, his legs in the air. He stayed in that silly position until Colter finally grinned and scratched his belly.

Sacagawea began nursing Pomp when she finished eating. Seaman crept softly beside her and rested a paw on her lap. She smiled and stroked his soft ears with her free hand. In a quiet voice, she sang a Shoshone lullaby.

The next day, they proceeded on. Dark circles rimmed the eyes of every man. Sacagawea wrapped her horse's reins around her hands and gripped them tightly, afraid she would faint and tumble to the ground. As they rode, she slipped Pomp off her back and nursed him, wondering how long her milk would hold out. That evening, York made a big pot of soup from the leftovers of the horse meat.

On September 22, Seaman again dashed ahead of the group. Lewis heard him barking in the distance. The captain reined in his horse to listen. Was he imagining something? That sounded like the bark Seaman always gave when he greeted one of the men. Lewis squinted, trying to see through the brush. He nudged his horse ahead eagerly.

In a few minutes, Lewis's face opened into a smile as wide as the western sky. One of Clark's hunters was running toward them, with Seaman prancing along beside him. The hunter carried a big pack on his back. Lewis jumped off his horse and clasped the hunter's shoulders.

"Captain Clark and the advance group are in an Indian village," the man announced breathlessly. "It's only seven and a half miles from here!" He slipped off his pack and revealed its treasures to Lewis. "I've got plenty of dried fish and roots in here. Captain Clark wanted me to bring you this food as soon as I could. I ran most of the way up the trail."

Lewis patted the fellow's back and ordered a fire to be prepared. His group was weak from hunger. They would eat before they made their way to the village.

As Lewis ate, he reflected on the events of the last few weeks. Since leaving their camp at Travelers' Rest, the explorers had covered more than 150 grueling miles in eleven days. They had made it across the Rocky Mountains! The starving time was over!

That evening, Lewis's group straggled into the Indian village.

They were cold, ragged, and worn-out. Their horses looked like walking skeletons with matted fur stretched over bones. But the men's faces were radiant—they had crossed the western mountains and lived to tell about it!

Curious Nez Perce Indians came out to greet the newcomers. The first white men these villagers had ever seen were the members of Clark's advance group. The villagers offered Lewis's group food—dried fish and berries, as well as cakes made from the ground-up root of the camas, a local lily. Of course, the explorers gratefully accepted the food. They sat down to a second meal in a single day—an unbelievable luxury!

As they feasted, Seaman jumped to his feet and began to bark. He dashed off into the darkness beyond the campfire, returning with Captain Clark. Smiling, Clark rushed to Lewis, who rose to his feet. The captains clasped each other's shoulders and took a long look in each other's eyes. It was such a relief to be reunited!

Clark shook hands all around, slapping the men on their backs. "A job well done!" he told them proudly. "Every single member of the Corps made it across the mountains!"

When Clark got to Sacagawea, he paused. "It is good to see you," he told her warmly, like a father talking to a grown child. "I was worried about you and the baby." He held out his arms for Pomp. Sacagawea passed her seven-month-old son to the captain. Clark held him gently and nuzzled him, nose to nose. The baby gave a little laugh, and Clark beamed. "He doesn't look any the worse for his travels. This is a robust little adventurer, indeed!"

"I've just come from a meeting with the Nez Perce chiefs, Meriwether," Clark said, sitting down by the fire. Suddenly, he stopped and whirled around. Everybody was chewing, gulping, biting hungrily into the dried fish, the berries, and the camas cakes. "Stop!" he ordered. "Stop eating that food!"

The group stared at him, amazed. Didn't he realize how hungry they were? How little they had eaten in the past eleven days?

"But, William, surely—" Lewis began to protest.

"How much of the Nez Perce food have you already eaten today?" Clark interrupted. "Eat sparingly of it. It gives you a stomachache!" Clark turned to Lewis to explain. "Believe me, Meriwether, we learned the hard way. My men gorged themselves as soon as we reached this village. This is the only type of food the Indians have, and it doesn't seem to upset their stomachs. But we paid dearly for our appetites!"

Clark advised the explorers to eat just a little food at a time, until their pinched stomachs could accept this strange new diet.

But they had been so hungry for so many days! Here was food aplenty, and it was nearly impossible to resist just one more bite! Although the men trusted Clark's advice, they couldn't turn their backs on food when they were so hungry.

In a few hours, the explorers understood Clark's warning. First, their bellies began to bloat. They went to sleep with upset stomachs and awoke in the night with cramps. By morning, the cramping was severe. In a few hours, the vomiting began. That was followed by diarrhea. The symptoms continued through the next day. These men who had been so hungry couldn't stand the sight of food. For that matter, their stomach pains were so severe they could not stand at all!

Even Seaman got sick. He walked weakly to the edge of camp and nibbled on grass until he vomited. Then he padded back to the explorers, swaying with each step. All around him, men were lying on their bedrolls, moaning.

It had taken eleven days of near-starvation to cross the high mountains. It took many of the explorers longer to recuperate from their first food west of the Rocky Mountains!

CHAPTER ELEVEN

```
        N
    W --◇-- E
        S
```

OCEAN IN VIEW!
OH, THE JOY!

October through November 6, 1805

"**I** don't know why my stomach isn't as happy as the rest of me," York said thoughtfully. "'Cause the rest of me sure is pleased to be on the other side of those big mountains!"

George Shannon laughed and tossed a stick to Seaman, who caught it before it touched the ground. "Wait a couple of days," Shannon said. "Your stomach is still homesick for buffalo sausage and roasted deer meat."

York groaned. "Let's don't talk about food right now, Mr. George. As soon as I'm thinking I might want some, my stomach starts to ache again."

Seaman sat in front of Shannon, the stick in his mouth and his tail wagging. Seaman had already adjusted to the new diet of dried fish, roots, and berries. So had young Shannon and a few of the other men.

"You'll get used to the new foods soon," Shannon said.

Seaman padded around camp like a four-footed nurse. If a sick man groaned in misery, Seaman nuzzled the patient's face. Sometimes a dizzy man would call the dog over and make a shaky attempt to sit up by holding onto Seaman's big body. At night,

Seaman settled down beside Lewis, and the sick captain snuggled up to the dog's warm fur.

While recovering from their stomach troubles, the explorers camped near the Nez Perce village. The Indian squaws fed them. As soon as some of the men were healthy, the Indians pointed out the edible plants in this new country.

The Nez Perce Indians could not understand the languages spoken by any of the explorers, not even the Shoshone or Hidatsa languages of Sacagawea and Old Toby. Nor could they understand the explorers' sign language, the silent hand signals used by most of the Plains Indians to communicate between tribes. So the explorers and the Nez Perce developed their own simple hand signals. The Nez Perce advised the explorers about the route to the western sea by drawing pictures in the dirt or in the air.

Since the explorers had not carried their heavy boats across the mountains, they needed to begin making new canoes as soon as some of the men were strong enough to work. While Lewis recuperated, Clark gathered the healthiest members of the Corps for this task. Seaman jogged along between Shannon and Colter as they followed Twisted Hair, the old chief of the Nez Perce village. He led them to a spot where large ponderosa pine trees grew.

The explorers chose five thick, straight trees and cut them down. They chopped off the branches and stripped off the bark. Then Twisted Hair showed them how to make fires along the length of the tree trunks to burn out the wood in the center. The men camped by the fires and kept them burning day and night.

Seaman returned to the main camp to sleep beside Lewis during the night, but in the morning he ran through the cool woods to visit the men making canoes. The canoe camp smelled of pine needles and a wood fire.

One morning, Clark fastened the saddlebags around Seaman's back and packed some roots for the canoe-makers to eat. When Seaman bounded into the canoe camp, Shannon opened the saddlebags and found the roots. "Good boy, Seaman. You're the delivery dog for our camp!"

That evening, the canoe-makers sent a note back in Seaman's saddlebags to report that the boat-making was going quickly. Shannon had been amusing himself in the evenings by whittling a little toy for Pomp out of a scrap of the pine. It looked like a dog with a big head, thick fur, and small, hanging ears—a likeness of Seaman. He packed the toy in Seaman's saddlebags.

When Seaman returned to the main camp that night, Clark opened Seaman's saddlebags. He took out the little wooden dog and smiled. "Look, Janey," he said to Sacagawea, calling her by the nickname he had given her. "Here's a little Seaman for Pomp to play with."

Sacagawea showed the little carving to Pomp, who reached for it with two chubby hands. He waved it happily in the air and then stuck the wooden dog's legs in his mouth.

Finally, the canoes were finished. Using the Indian shortcut, the explorers had hollowed out five canoes in ten days. Most of the men were feeling better. The Corps of Discovery was ready to continue traveling.

The captains asked the villagers if they would care for the expedition's horses until the following spring when the explorers expected to return, and the Nez Perce agreed. Before leaving, the explorers branded their horses so they would be able to recognize them. Twisted Hair offered to go with the Corps as a guide through the lands of the Nez Perce. Since this mighty tribe and its relatives spread across many villages covering hundreds of miles, the captains eagerly accepted his offer.

Sliding their canoes into the Clearwater River, the explorers waved good-bye to the kindly Nez Perce villagers on the afternoon of October 7. They covered twenty miles before stopping for evening camp.

"Now this is my kind of travel!" York declared. "I just stick my paddle in the river and feel that current push us downstream. We are really moving! Like the birds in the sky, we just watch the trees go by!"

"You said it," Colter exclaimed. "We're moving more swiftly than any horse could run!"

The men were thrilled! This was the first time they had traveled with a river's current since leaving the Ohio River in November of 1803, almost two years earlier. They had forgotten how easy it was to paddle *with* the current.

Seaman sat near the bow of a canoe, stuck his furry face out, and gulped the wind. The shaggy fur on his chest blew in the wind. When he opened his mouth and let his tongue hang loosely, he looked like he was laughing. The sight of him made John Colter think of the delights of a hunt on a breezy fall day. It made Sacagawea remember her childhood, when she ran carefree along the banks of the Missouri. George Shannon simply wished he had been born a puppy!

The Shoshone guide, Old Toby, did not share the explorers' enthusiasm for the swiftly moving rivers. He clenched his jaw and sat, unsmiling, through a few days of river travel. His eyes looked longingly at the trees beside the river. He refused to speak when Sacagawea asked him if he was feeling well. Once, Seaman sat beside him and nuzzled his arm, but Old Toby clutched the side of the rocking boat and turned his face away.

Then, one evening, Old Toby ran off without saying good-bye or asking for his pay. The captains wanted to send a man after him to deliver his earnings and their thanks for guiding them through the Rocky Mountains. But Twisted Hair advised them to let the poor fellow go.

Captain Lewis was still feeling weak and sickly. He sat beside Seaman in the canoe and leaned against the dog's warm, solid body. As Seaman sniffed the air, Lewis dozed.

On October 10, the Corps camped where the Clearwater River flows into the Snake River. Local Indians sold the explorers dried fish and dog meat. Most of the men thought the dog meat tasted delicious because it was more tender than elk or deer meat. Captain Lewis was just regaining his appetite, and he relished the meat. The only member of the group who found the dog meat distasteful was Captain Clark. Although he longed for the taste of meat, Clark just could not get used to the idea of eating dog meat.

By the time the canoes reached a long stretch of rapids on October 13, Lewis's energy had returned.

"What do you think, Meriwether?" Clark asked, as they walked along the riverbank to survey the rapids below them. "Can the canoes make it through this whitewater? Or should we portage?"

Lewis studied the foamy water rushing downstream. "I think we can steer around the boulders, and I don't see any big drops. Let's try it," Lewis said. "We've been making such good progress, and the men are eager to reach the sea. A portage will slow us down."

Clark looked at the swift whitewater and hesitated. "We've got a lot to lose in these rapids, Meriwether. If we portage, all we have to lose is a little time."

"Let me try it with two of the canoes. If I can make it through, then you follow with the rest."

Clark was still undecided.

"We won't put the nonswimmers on the lead canoes," Lewis urged. "Or the journals and the most valuable baggage. And I'll take Seaman with me. If one of the canoes capsizes, he'll pull the men to shore."

Clark was doubtful, but he agreed to give it a try. His group, which included the nonswimmers and Charbonneau's family, watched as the first two canoes slid into the rushing water. Clark paid careful attention to the route the lead canoes took through the rapids, paddling around boulders and gliding over small drops. When the first group ran smoothly through the rapids, Clark's group eagerly ran for their canoes.

As soon as Lewis's boats were past the rapids, they pulled to shore to wait for Clark's group. While Clark led the three remaining canoes into the river, Lewis walked back upstream with Seaman, a few strong swimmers, and some ropes. They ran along the banks as Clark's canoes rode the rapids so they could help if there was a mishap. But Clark's canoes ran the rapids without any problem.

The canoes seemed to fly downstream on the Snake River, passing between stark canyon walls and through swift, bubbling rapids. Every time the explorers ran the rapids, they were taking dangerous chances. The dugout canoes did not handle well. They overturned easily, took in water, and slammed against rocks. Sometimes baggage was damaged or pieces fell out. But the men were delighted with their speed so they were willing to take risks.

The group passed the villages of the Nez Perce and their relatives, the Yakima and Wallawalla Indians. These tribes were part of the same Indian nation, and they spoke a language similar to the Nez Perce. All of these Indians welcomed the explorers because of their guide, Twisted Hair. The captains held meetings with the chiefs of these villages, gave speeches, and passed out medals.

Since the Corps of Discovery had passed beyond the boundaries of the Louisiana Purchase, the explorers were no longer in the territory owned by the United States. In fact, none of the white men's nations claimed this land. The captains hoped to establish trade between their country and these Indians before England, Canada, or Spain was able to make contacts. Indeed, the explorers were establishing trade as they passed. It would slow their progress to send out hunters, so the captains traded with the Indians for food.

The Corps of Discovery was moving faster than it had ever traveled before. Everybody's spirits were high. In the evenings, Cruzatte played his fiddle around the campfire, and the men danced. Local Indians joined them for these parties. York danced his jigs to the delight of the Indians of the West.

Sacagawea let Pomp crawl between the men seated around the campfire. The eight-month-old baby had just figured out how to creep around, and he gurgled with pride whenever he was allowed to test his new skill. As soon as Sacagawea put the baby on the ground, Seaman moved to his side. The big dog positioned himself between the fire and the child. If Pomp started to crawl beyond the ring of people seated around the campfire, Seaman nudged him back into the circle.

Captain Clark loved to watch little Pomp. "Your son is a born explorer, Janey," he said to Sacagawea. "But he'll never explore any farther than the campfire if Seaman has his way. Look at how that dog keeps an eye on him! Who would think a dog that hunts as well as a wolf would become a tender-hearted nursemaid at the sight of a baby?"

Lewis smiled. "Why, William, I believe we could say the same thing about you! You've got such a soft spot for this baby—I wouldn't be surprised if you find yourself a wife and become a family man just as soon as we step foot back in the United States."

On October 15, the explorers could see mountains in the distance. The next day, the Corps of Discovery reached another river. According to Twisted Hair, this was the mighty river that flowed into the Pacific Ocean. The captains knew this must be the Columbia River from reports of United States sea captains who sailed to the west coast of North America.

"Look here, Meriwether!" called Clark. "This river is so clear you can see pebbles, even grains of sand on its bottom!"

The group made camp for two days to explore the area around this famed river. Now that they had reached the Columbia River, they knew they would be able to find the western sea.

"Feast your eyes on all that salmon!" exclaimed Lewis, looking into the river. "Have you ever seen so many fish?"

Most of the salmon had just spawned and were dead or dying. But Seaman splashed into the river and swam downstream. When he returned, he was holding a large, wiggling salmon. He shook the water off his coat, then trotted over to York, carrying the treasure proudly in his mouth.

"You get me a couple more of these big, juicy ones, Seaman," York said, kneeling to take the fish.

Seaman wagged his tail, his tongue hanging out and his bright eyes focused on York's face. He looked like he was grinning.

"Mmmn, mmmn. We're going to have some fresh fish with our supper tonight! Fried crispy on the outside, and juicy on the inside. Now that will be some fine eating!" York pointed at the river. "Go ahead, Seaman. Get me some more of these fish."

Seaman woofed happily and bounded back into the river.

One evening, some local Indians came to trade with the explorers. A brave was wearing a sailor's jacket. Lewis touched the sleeve of the jacket and raised his shoulders to ask where the man had bought it.

The Indian drew a picture in the dirt with a stick. Lewis stood beside the brave, cupping his chin in his hand as he watched the drawing take shape. Seaman stood next to Lewis, following the movements of the stick in the Indian's fingers. The drawing looked like a rough outline of a ship with masts. The captains' eyes met. Were they close enough to the Pacific Ocean for the local Indians to trade with sailing ships?

When the Indian finished his drawing, Twisted Hair questioned him. Yes, Twisted Hair nodded to the captains. The jacket had come from white men who sailed the big waters—the Pacific Ocean.

The captains beamed. They were nearing the western sea!

On October 23, the explorers encountered a wild section of rapids and waterfalls on the Columbia River.

"I'm not surprised, Meriwether," Clark said. "If we're getting close to the Pacific Ocean, the Columbia River has to drop quickly to sea level."

Lewis nodded. "Let's have a look at the river and decide whether we can send the boats through."

The captains took Seaman for a walk beside the noisy river. They had to shout so their voices could be heard over the sound of the rushing water. They discovered a waterfall nearly forty feet high and made plans to portage around it. The captains decided they could run most of the rapids. But in some of the rougher spots, the men would need to empty the canoes and lower them by ropes through the rapids while standing on the banks. As soon as the canoes were in safer waters, the men would refill them with baggage and passengers and proceed on.

Indians gathered on the riverbanks to watch the explorers run their canoes through each section of rapids. These Indians were from a tribe called the Chinooks, and they did not look, dress, or speak like Twisted Hair's people. They were shorter, with large, flat feet and pointed heads. On their upper bodies, they wore fur pieces, short robes, and beads around their necks, arms, and legs. Most of them wore nothing else except a small skin tied around their waists and between their legs. According to Twisted Hair, the Chinooks were not friendly with the Nez Perce.

As the Corps continued down the Columbia River, the Chinooks visited the explorers' camps, eager to trade. These Indians made wonderful canoes that were lighter than the explorers' dugouts, yet sturdier and easier to navigate. Lewis managed to purchase one of the Chinook canoes by offering the smallest of the expedition's dugout canoes as well as several other items, including a hatchet.

The next section of rapids was a quarter mile of swirling water that swelled between rocky ledges. The captains packed their most valuable items on the nonswimmers' backs and told them to scramble alongside the river. The other explorers, along with the heaviest baggage, would take their chances in the canoes.

Hundreds of Chinooks gathered on the banks to watch.

"Why are all those Indians standing along the banks?" York asked. "They make me nervous." He looked at the river ahead. "And I don't need any help feeling nervous when I see that water leaping and roaring below me."

Colter looked at the crowd of Indian spectators. "You know why they're watching us, York. They think we're crazy to run these rapids." Colter grinned. "They think our canoes will end up in splinters, and all our baggage will wash downstream. After we break our fool necks, the Chinooks will shake their heads at our stupidity and gather up what's left of our belongings for their own use!"

York scowled. "These Indians live here and ride around in canoes all the time. If they think it's crazy to run these rapids, why are we going to try it?"

"Maybe because we *are* crazy!" Colter called merrily, as he pushed one of the canoes into the frothy water. He nodded at the others in his canoe and dug in his paddle.

As the roar of the whitewater swallowed their voices, York thought he heard Colter whoop like a boy diving happily into a cool pool on a hot summer day.

York shook his head, smiling. "Maybe we are crazy, I don't know," he muttered. "That John Colter is crazy, for sure. As crazy as they come! That man, he eats danger for his supper!"

Lewis stood on a ledge above the river while the canoes swept through the rapids. He held a rope coiled in his hand, and he kept Seaman by his side. If a boat overturned, the passengers would desperately need Seaman's help to pull them to safety.

To everybody's amazement, none of the canoes splintered on the rocks. Lewis, Seaman, and the Chinook Indians watched all the canoes run the rapids without loss of life or baggage.

For the next few miles, the river was fairly calm, then began a three-mile stretch of wild water. Again, the Chinooks gathered along the banks to watch the disaster. Again, the explorers made it.

After these rapids, the Corps camped for three days to dry out and repair the dents and leaks in their canoes. The captains named the place Fort Rock Camp. At this camp, Twisted Hair said good-bye. He was no longer able to help them trade with the Indians, since they had left the lands of the Nez Perce nation. The

explorers would be able find their way to the western sea by staying on the Columbia River. It was time for Twisted Hair to return
to his own village.

On October 29, the Corps of Discovery proceeded on, reaching
the next section of rapids on the last day of the month. This was
the most frightening section of river the explorers had ever seen.
It was four miles long and full of waterfalls! When Captain Clark
wrote about it in his journal, he described "great numbers of
both large and Small rocks, water passing with great velocity
forming & boiling in a most horriable manner, with a fall of about
20 feet...."

It took two full days to get the canoes through these rapids. The
explorers portaged around the worst of the falls and lowered
empty canoes with ropes through the worst of the rapids.
Whenever the men thought they could run the rapids, they hopped
aboard and rode the foamy, gushing water, paddling around boulders and avoiding dead trees that could snag the boats.

"We did it, William!" Lewis exclaimed when the canoes were in
calm water again. "We made it through four miles of rapids without any injuries. We didn't lose a single canoe!"

The next day, the Corps awakened to fog. The canoes reached
Beacon Rock, which marks the beginning of the Columbia River's
tidewater. From that point on, ocean tides sweeping into the
mouth of the river cause the river waters to rise and fall.

On November 4, the Corps made camp near the mouth of the
Willamette River. Sea captains had come this far inland on the
Columbia River, and they had described the area in their writings.
So the expedition was now in territory that had been explored
and mapped by English speakers.

Clark beamed. "For the first time since Fort Mandan, we have
a real map to guide us!" he announced. "Not just a drawing in the
dirt, but a *real* map with English words."

As the explorers continued moving west, the Columbia River
began to widen. It was becoming an estuary, a section of river

...*water passing with great velocity forming & boiling in a most horriable manner....*

—Journal of Captain William Clark, October 31, 1805

where the sea's saltwater mixes with the river's freshwater. The climate in the estuary was different from that of the upper Columbia. The sky was cloudy most days, and it rained often. A thick cover of plants lined the banks below tall, needle-bearing trees. Ducks and gulls swam noisily by the canoes. Swans glided gracefully through the waters.

The Chinook Indians lived in villages along the riverbanks. They were eager to trade, and they often visited the explorers' camps with roots, fish, and meat.

"It's gone!" Colter muttered one evening, after a group of Chinook traders had visited the explorers' camp.

"What's gone?" Shannon asked.

"My tin cup. I left it right here, on top of my pack. Those Indians were standing here, showing Captain Lewis a basket of roots they wanted to trade. I walked over to the fire to see if the water was hot, and when I came back my cup was gone." Colter frowned. "And the Chinook traders are gone, too. Have you noticed how our things seem to disappear after those Indians pay a visit to our camp?"

Shannon and Colter looked into the darkness around the camp. "They're long gone, John. You'll never catch up with them in the dark."

Colter sucked in his breath and clenched his fists. "Every time we turn around, those Indians steal something."

"It sure is frustrating," Shannon agreed. "They come into our camp, charge us outrageous prices for their food, and walk off with anything they can find. But it's not worth stopping to fight with them. Just forget it, John."

The Corps of Discovery kept moving west toward the ocean. Paddling as rapidly as they could, the explorers covered thirty miles each day. On November 7, when the fog cleared, the explorers saw such a vast expanse of water before them that they thought they had arrived at the Pacific Ocean. The waves rocked their canoes and crashed against distant rocks. Seagulls squawked overhead.

"Hooray!" the men shouted. "We've reached the western sea!" They lifted their paddles into the air and cheered, making the canoes teeter on the waves. Seaman jumped to his feet, barking at the commotion. The men grinned and hugged each other.

Colter leaped into the water, and Seaman jumped in after him. The two splashed in the cold water until the captains called them back to the boats. That evening, Captain Clark wrote in his field notes: "Ocian in view! O! the joy."

CHAPTER TWELVE

A SOGGY WINTER

November 7, 1805, through March 23, 1806

The next day, the explorers glimpsed land across the water. Puzzled, the men studied the horizon. How could they see land across the water if they were on the coast of the Pacific Ocean? Lewis stood up for a better look.

"We haven't reached the coast," Lewis announced as he scanned the horizon. "We're still in the Columbia estuary."

The men's excitement faded. The estuary had become so wide, and the pull of the tides had become so strong that the explorers had been fooled into thinking they had reached the sea. But they had made a mistake. Discouraged, they continued paddling west.

Each morning the men pushed off their canoes eagerly, expecting to reach the Pacific Ocean that day. The explorers could taste salt in the estuary water, and the salty taste grew stronger each day. After Seaman swam, his fur felt sticky and smelled like sea brine. When his fur dried, white salt clung to the ends of his black fur like the silvery tips of grizzly bear fur.

The skies became stormy and gusts of wind rocked the canoes. Sacagawea and several men became seasick.

The cloudy, windy weather continued, dampening the men's enthusiasm as well as their supplies. York remarked, "I thought the word 'pacific' meant calm. Peaceful."

Clark nodded. "It does."

"Then whoever named this ocean must have been stupid. He needed to study the meaning of his words."

Clark smiled.

"Just look at this water," York said. "All the time crashing. We haven't even reached the open ocean, but the waves are already so big they make me sick to my stomach. And it's so noisy! There's nothing peaceful about the Pacific Ocean."

"I suppose the person who named this ocean was here in summertime," Clark commented. "It's fall now. Seas always get stormy in fall. Even back East."

"Well, maybe the western sea is pacific in summertime. But right now, it seems plain old nasty," York complained. "And I don't like the feel of it, neither. It rots away my clothes. Look at how this shirt is falling apart." York held up his arm to show the tattered sleeve of his buckskin shirt.

The sea air seeped into skin and fur as well as clothing, so the explorers always felt damp and clammy. After he swam in the estuary, Seaman's fur was sticky. When it dried, his hair matted into stiff clumps. Sacagawea tried to untangle the dog's fur by combing it with a smooth stick, but the mats formed again as soon as Seaman went swimming.

Once their canoes had entered the Columbia estuary, the explorers rarely found a comfortable spot to camp. Often, they had to huddle in a small cove with barely enough space for everybody to keep their toes dry! They slept on beds of pebbles. Gusts of chilly, damp wind blew against their faces, and pounding surf assaulted their ears. Fires were hard to start and even harder to keep going. The ground smelled like decaying sea animals.

On November 10, the boats pulled into Point Ellice, on the north bank of the Columbia Estuary. The explorers thought they had found a good campsite because high cliffs at the back of the beach would shelter them from some of the wind. But a storm at sea sent waves and high winds to batter the shore. The waves were so strong the explorers could not get their boats back out, and Point Ellice became a prison. It rained for eleven days. High tide was a horror—the waves drove gigantic uprooted trees crashing into camp. Captain Clark described their misery in his journal: "The wind increased to a Storm...throwing the water of the river with emence waves out of its banks almost over whelming us....O! how horriable is the day."

One afternoon while the explorers were stranded at Point Ellice, Seaman stood at the edge of the water and began to bark. The men spotted a dark shape bobbing up, then vanishing behind the waves. The shape gradually came nearer, and they could see it was a boat. Indians were rowing out to the stranded explorers! They were Clatsops, relatives of the Chinooks. The short, half-naked Indians pulled their canoe onto Point Ellice beach and unloaded baskets of roots and fish. The captains and Seaman gathered around the canoe. Gratefully, the explorers purchased the Clatsops' food.

If the Clatsops could get in and out of Point Ellice during the stormy weather, perhaps some of the stronger men could manage to get out. On November 13, the captains sent off Colter, Shannon, and another man in the expedition's Indian canoe.

The next day, Seaman ran to the rocks at the back of the beach, barking excitedly. He scrambled up the rocks and tunneled into the thick underbrush. A few minutes later, he trotted back beside John Colter.

"We found a sandy beach on the bay," Colter reported. "There's some game over there, too."

Everybody was relieved. As soon as they could, the explorers moved to the more comfortable campsite.

The captains were hoping to meet a seagoing ship as they neared the coast. Before the expedition started, President Jefferson had given Captain Lewis a letter so the Corps could purchase goods on credit. If the explorers could find a seagoing ship from the United States, they would be able to restock their supplies for their return trip.

But the nearer the expedition got to the ocean, the more difficult travel became because of the tides and stormy weather. Instead of taking the whole expedition to the coast, the captains decided to send small scouting parties to search for seagoing vessels. The rest of the Corps camped along the estuary. The scouting parties went up the Pacific coast for several miles. They visited Indian villages along the coast. But none of the local Indians could offer any information about a ship docked in the area.

"My guess is we arrived too late to catch any seagoing vessels," Clark reported, after he returned from a scouting trip on foot along the coast. "It's November, and the stormy season has certainly started here. Most seagoing ships leave by October."

Lewis nodded. "We'd better start building our fort. We can't camp in this miserable rain all winter."

The captains discussed the location for their winter fort. They needed a spot with fresh water for drinking, timber for building, and enough game for food. Local Indians reported that elk were more plentiful south of the Columbia Estuary. But perhaps the Corps should make camp along the seacoast in the hope a ship might come by? Then again, the coastal climate was so wet that it might be better to travel back up the Columbia River and build a fort near the Nez Perce or their relatives. That would also give the Corps a head start on their homeward journey.

The captains called the entire group together. Seaman lay between the captains as they spoke.

"We're going to take a vote on where we build our winter camp," Lewis announced, looking at each of the explorers. "There are good reasons for each course of action. If we camp close to the sea, we might meet up with a ship from our country, and we'll be able to restock the trade goods for our return voyage. But it's wet and stormy by the coast."

As Lewis spoke, Seaman held his head high, watching. Lewis's cheeks were pink from the damp wind, and his hair whipped around his face. Some of the explorers held their hands in front of their eyes to protect them from the blowing sand. Sacagawea draped her blanket over her head and shoulders so Pomp would stay warm and dry in his cradleboard on her back.

"We can also build our winter quarters inland," Clark said. "That will put us under the shelter of the trees. If we build in the woods north of the estuary, the Chinook Indians will be our neighbors. If we choose the south side of the Columbia, we'll live near the Clatsops. Both groups are peaceful and eager to trade with us."

Seaman felt a tickle on his side and scratched at a flea with his hind paw. He looked at the human explorers. As they listened to the captains, most of them were also scratching their hair or rubbing their tattered clothes against their itchy skin. Seaman chewed at the fur on one of his front legs, trying to bite off another pesky flea.

"It might be best to head back up the Columbia River and spend the winter near the Nez Perce nation," Clark was saying. "They have our horses, and they welcomed us with great kindness after we crossed the Rockies."

"We want everyone in the Corps to have a voice in this decision," Lewis said. "Let's talk about the advantages of each location."

Every adult in the group was included in the decision, even York and Sacagawea. This was remarkable, for in 1805, black men, like York, were not allowed to vote in United States elections. Nor were Indians or women, like Sacagawea.

After some discussion and a show of hands, the group voted to build their fort inland, on the southern side of the Columbia

Estuary. On November 26, the explorers got back into their canoes and paddled south. Lewis took Seaman and a few men to search for a suitable spot.

When his group returned, Lewis announced, "We found a place for our fort, William. It's near a spring with fresh drinking water. There are lots of trees and plenty of game—the men killed six elk and five deer in the area."

"Is it far from the ocean?" Clark asked. "We should set up an operation to boil seawater so we'll have a supply of salt."

"Not far, just a few miles from the coast," Lewis answered. "There's a river near the spot, but the fort will be up on a bluff so we shouldn't be in danger of flooding."

"Sounds good to me," Clark said. He leaned over to stroke the matted fur under Seaman's ears. "You ready to move into a fort so we can get out of the rain, Seaman? I know I am."

The Corps of Discovery began building Fort Clatsop on December 8. During construction, it rained almost every day. The men felled trees and stripped the branches off the trunks. They pushed the trunks into the soft earth to form the fort's outer walls. Seaman helped the men carry branches and brush to the edge of the clearing. He dragged the branches in his mouth and made a game of the work by racing the men to the brushpiles. Water streamed off the men's faces as they worked, and Seaman's coat dripped. He shook off every few minutes, but nobody shooed him away because everything was already wet.

"Again the rain," muttered Charbonneau one day. "I think more water falls on Fort Clatsop than fills the whole Pacific Ocean!"

Shannon grinned. "Cheer up, man! We struggled for a year and a half to reach this place. We'd better make the best of it now that we're finally here."

On December 23, the captains carried their bedrolls into their unfinished quarters. Seaman padded around the new building, sniffing the fresh pine floors, rough writing tables, and log walls.

Lewis unrolled his blankets, and Seaman stretched out beside him. This was going to be home for the winter.

The next day, the men finished covering most of the other buildings inside Fort Clatsop's walls. They carried their gear into new, dry sleeping quarters.

At dawn on December 25, Seaman scrambled to his feet. The men were gathered outside the captains' hut. They fired a volley, shouted, and sang to announce Christmas Day, 1805.

Lewis rolled over and hid his face with his arm, but Seaman tugged at his covers until Lewis hoisted himself up on an elbow.

"Merry Christmas, Seaman!" Lewis said, laughing.

Clark rolled out of his damp sleeping roll and sat up. "Good morning, Meriwether." He shouted to the men outside, "Here we are at Fort Clatsop, men. The Corps of Discovery has reached the Pacific Ocean. Now that's a fine Christmas present!"

Seaman swabbed Clark's face with his tongue, then dragged the rest of the covers off Lewis. The captains were much too slow moving this morning so Seaman ran out the open doorway to join the carolers.

The group feasted on good wishes. There wasn't much else. It was a holiday for hunters as well as builders, and in the damp climate, meat and fish went rotten quickly. So the menu for Christmas dinner was spoiled elk meat, rotting fish, and a few soggy roots. The meat and fish smelled so bad that the men had to force themselves to put the food in their mouths. Seaman was not as fussy as the human explorers. He was the only member of the Corps who ate with an appetite.

After Christmas Day, the men completed work on a smoke-house to dry and preserve their meat. Fort Clatsop was finished in time for the new year.

January 1, 1806, was damp and drizzly. The explorers hardly celebrated the New Year's Day at all. But at least the fort was finished, so they had dry wood floors to sleep on and a roof to keep the constant rain off them.

As soon as the explorers moved into their new quarters, so did the fleas. Even cheerful Shannon grumbled about these pests. "These tiny little varmints are more troublesome than mosquitoes, ticks, and gnats combined!" he complained. "It's bad enough they eat me alive. Why do they have to wake me up in the night to devour me? I think I slept better on the prickly pears back at Great Falls!"

"It doesn't seem to freeze out here in winter, so the fleas don't get killed off," Colter said. "You just have to ignore them, Shannon, or you'll scratch your skin raw. Like poor Seaman is doing."

The men looked at Seaman, who was scratching his side with his hind leg. The dog jumped up, then plopped right back down to scratch the other side. Day after day, he scratched. He rolled onto his back and slid along the rough boards to scratch his itchy skin. He dug through his fur with his snout, trying to bite off the itchy little creatures. Sometimes he chewed off clumps of hair, exposing raw patches of skin. Sacagawea rubbed grease on the sores, but Seaman licked off the grease and chewed off more fur.

The winter weather at Fort Clatsop was either damp and drab or wet and gusty. Although it was never very cold, it was also never very sunny. Between early December and late March, the explorers counted only six days of fair weather and only twelve days without rain.

Most days, the hunters went out in search of game. They returned with damp clothes and wet moccasins. Seaman's coat got soaked when he went hunting with the men because the ground was always soggy, and the trees dripped.

Usually, the hunters brought back elk, so most of the meals at Fort Clatsop were elk. Boiled elk. Dried elk. Jerked elk. Sometimes spoiled elk. In three months, the explorers consumed 131 elk. When the men returned from hunting, they hurried to smoke any extra game before it started to spoil. As winter wore on, the hunters killed all the game in the nearby countryside. The captains had to trade with the Clatsop Indians for fish, roots, and dog meat to add to their food supplies.

When the men weren't hunting, they spent their days inside the damp fort scraping elk hides, sewing moccasins for the return trip, and stoking the smokehouse fire. For outdoorsmen, these were boring tasks. The gloomy skies made everybody feel gloomy. Even Seaman padded through the fort with a drooping tail. The men complained of colds, flu, and muscle strains.

Much of the captains' time at Fort Clatsop was taken up with their writing. They sat on rough benches, bent over crude desks, and wrote by candlelight. Seaman stretched out on the floor in the captains' quarters and watched them dip their quill pens into bottles of ink and scratch them across pages and pages. Lewis described plants, animals, and Indians. Clark made a careful map of the lands they had traveled through. He estimated they had covered over four thousand miles from the mouth of the Missouri River to the Pacific Ocean! His estimate was based on his daily count of the miles by "dead reckoning"— by comparing the distance from one point to the next based on a similar but known distance.

"Have you noticed how well the Indian hats shed water?" Lewis said to Clark one day as they sat in their quarters, writing. He was describing the hats in his notes. "They're so tightly woven that water rolls off the cedar bark. I'd like to have one of those hats."

Clark laughed. "Watch out! It will probably cost more than you want to spend!"

"The Clatsops do charge awfully steep prices," Lewis said, shaking his head. "They always get the better deal in a trade."

"But at least they're honest," Clark said. "When the Chinooks came to our camp to trade, they were always stealing things. I haven't heard any of our men complaining about the Clatsops stealing from the fort."

"The Clatsops have some admirable qualities. They know how to make wonderful canoes," Lewis continued, reflecting aloud about this tribe. "Of all the Indians we've met, they seem the most peaceful. Their young men don't show any interest in fighting among themselves or with neighboring tribes."

"But some of their customs puzzle me, Meriwether."

Lewis nodded. "You're thinking about the way they flatten their babies' heads by keeping them between boards?"

"Yes," Clark answered, "it puzzles me that the Clatsops would consider a flattened head more beautiful. It also puzzles me that they admire stout legs on their women. So much so, they tie cords around their women's ankles to cause their legs to swell."

Lewis grinned mischievously. "I take it you're not planning to show your ladyfriend, Miss Julia, how to thicken her legs by binding her ankles," Lewis teased, "when we get back to the United States."

As soon as Lewis mentioned the name of this young woman, Clark's face turned as red as his hair. To hide his embarassment, Clark quickly dipped his pen into his bottle of ink and stooped over the map he was drawing. Seaman heard the playful tone in Lewis's voice and scrambled to his feet. He padded over to Lewis, a pinecone in his mouth and his tail wagging hopefully.

"All right, Seaman," Lewis said, taking the pinecone. "Let's go outside for awhile. I think William might prefer to be alone." He cleared his throat. "Alone with the map of his heart!"

Lewis chuckled at his own joke, closed his ink bottle, and skipped out the door of the captain's sleeping hut, with Seaman romping beside him. Clark kept his eyes on his paper, but the corners of his mouth curled into a little smile. On these gloomy days, he did catch himself feeling a bit homesick. And when his thoughts wandered toward the United States, he found himself picturing the young woman he hoped to marry.

The Clatsop Indians often came to the fort, and the explorers visited the nearby Indian village. The Clatsops lived in wooden houses divided into rooms for related families. When Seaman went with the men to the Indian village, he was welcome in the Indians' dim, smoky houses. The houses smelled like fish, because the Clatsops ate mostly fish, rather than meat. Large, decorated baskets filled with roots and seeds lined the walls of the houses. The likeable, easygoing Indian braves invited the explorers to play games, gamble, and smoke with them. Seaman dozed beside the men or retrieved sticks thrown by the Indian children.

One day, the Indians brought news to the fort—a whale had washed ashore! The captains decided to send a group to the coast to see this creature and bring back some meat. Captain Clark wanted to lead the group.

Sacagawea asked if she could go along on the trip. Her face fell when Clark said no.

"Janey," he explained, "you and little Pomp will be safer here. We're going to take a canoe over to the coast, and a storm might blow up at sea. Your baby is only eleven months old. He could slip off your back in rough waters. You remember how strong the waves were at Point Ellice? Remember how seasick you got riding over the waves?"

Sacagawea stood silently, looking at Clark. Seaman brushed against her leg, but she ignored him. Puzzled, Seaman sat and watched the Indian woman's face, his ears cocked.

"Besides," Clark continued, "we'll want big, strong men to butcher the whale carcass and haul the meat back to camp."

"I think it very hard to refuse me," Sacagawea said. "I have traveled a long way to see the great waters—as far as any of the men. And I have done my share of the work. Now, there is a monstrous fish to be seen. I wish very much to see it."

The captains' eyes met. This was the first time the Indian woman had been insistent about anything. She had traveled as far and worked as hard as any of them—perhaps more so, because she carried her child on her back. It did seem mean to deny her request.

...found only the Skelleton of this monster on the Sand...where the waves and tide had driven up & left it. this Skeleton measured 105 feet.

—Journal of Captain William Clark, January 8, 1806

Lewis nodded at Clark, then he spoke. "Janey and the baby have been on the canoes when we rode through some very rough rapids. She's been levelheaded in plenty of risky situations. I think she and Pomp will be safe at the seacoast," Lewis said. "This will probably be her only chance to see the Pacific Ocean."

Lewis added, "You can take Seaman along with you. He'll keep an eye on Pomp if the waves swamp the boat. As a matter of fact, Seaman would probably enjoy a romp by the ocean. He got his name because he was meant to go to the sea, and he hasn't been to the actual seacoast yet."

Clark agreed, and the party set off. They found the whale on the sandy beach near a creek on Tillamook Head on January 8. By the time they got there, the whale's blubber had already been removed by the Indians. But the huge skeleton lying on the sand was still an impressive sight.

"Look at this creature!" Clark exclaimed. "It's bigger than a house."

Seaman ran around the carcass, growling at its strange odor. He sniffed the whale's mouth and tugged at chunks of sandy skin.

Then he rolled in the wet sand, covering his own scent with the odor of dead sea life.

Captain Clark paced out the length of the skeleton and declared it was 105 feet long. The explorers walked around the carcass, amazed. They measured the thickness of the whale's bones by comparing them with the size of their hands. They knelt in the sand and brushed off the big tail to admire it.

Seaman wiggled inside the whale's ribs and barked playfully at the men. Pomp watched the dog from his clean, dry perch on Sacagawea's back. He laughed aloud when Seaman tunneled out of the skeleton and dashed past, flinging wet sand behind him.

The men visited local Indians to barter for blubber and whale oil. Sacagawea walked along the shore with Seaman.

From the beach, the gray, cloudy sky seemed endless. Out in the deeper water, large waves rolled and crashed. Yet when the same waves neared the shore, they grabbed softly at the wet sand under Sacagawea's bare feet. She stood facing the open ocean, thinking about the large world. She wondered if she was the first Shoshone woman who had stood at the edge of the Pacific Ocean.

Seaman splashed into the shallow water and pawed at a crab tumbling in the waves. Sacagawea smiled and slipped Pomp off her back. She held the baby at the edge of the water. He kicked his feet, squealing at the cold, moving water. Seaman dashed over, kicking a spray of water into the air, and nuzzled Pomp's face.

The big dog turned and leaped into the waves to grab a long ribbon of seaweed. He shook his head, waving the kelp in the air. Pomp laughed. Seaman turned and ran back to Pomp, dragging the seaweed. When the slimy kelp brushed against Pomp's hands, he gasped and started to cry. Sacagawea giggled and playfully splashed Seaman. Seaman dropped the seaweed and ran in a big circle around Sacagawea and Pomp, spraying water all over them.

Clark called to them. Sacagawea put Pomp back in his cradleboard and joined the group. The men had bought about three hundred pounds of blubber and oil to take back to Fort Clatsop. Clark cut off a chunk of pink-white blubber and offered it to Seaman. He wagged his tail, drooling, and swallowed the whole piece in one gulp.

Clark was very pleased with their whale of an adventure. In his journal, he wrote: "...thank providence for directing the whale to us; and think him much more kind to us than he was to jonah, having Sent this monster to be *Swallowed by us* in Sted of *Swallowing of us* as jonah's did."

The explorers were delighted to have a new food to vary their daily menu. They thought the blubber was very tender, with a slightly sweet taste. Shannon declared it was better than dog meat. York said the blubber tasted even better than beaver.

By March, the explorers were restless to be moving again. They hoped the winter snow and ice along their inland route had begun to melt so that travel would be easy. The men knew they would have to haul their canoes up the Columbia's rapids, and they had to reach the Rocky Mountains before the short summer in the high country was over. Once past these obstacles, they would be in the rich beaver and buffalo country of the Plains. Then they would be nearing St. Louis and home.

The captains were disappointed that they had not made contact with a seagoing vessel at the coast. That meant the Corps of Discovery would start home in a state of poverty, with only a handful of trade goods. But staying longer at Fort Clatsop would not help the situation, since the local Indians refused to lower their prices even though the expedition had almost nothing left to trade. During their last season of travel, the explorers had deposited several caches of supplies along their route. If those caches had not been raided, the captains hoped to pick up supplies and trade goods as they traveled.

As the men packed for the trip home, their excitement grew. They gathered their rifles and ammunition, kettles and tools, scientific instruments and journals. Seaman ran back and forth from the fort to the river, his saddlebags stuffed with gear.

"Hey, Seaman!" called York, as they walked up to the fort to get another load. He held out a sturdy stick for a game of tug of war. "Let's see who's stronger—the mighty York or the great Newfoundland."

Seaman grabbed the stick and shook his head from side to side. In less than a minute, the Newfoundland was holding the stick in his mouth, and York was pulling splinters out of his palm.

John Colter smirked as he walked by with a large box of supplies in his arms. "The mighty York is strong, all right!"

"Aw, that old stick was rotten," York muttered. "It fell apart in my hand." York pulled out splinters. "Everything gets rotten in this soppy weather."

Colter called over his shoulder, "The faster we get packed, the faster we get out of this soppy weather."

George Shannon jogged up from the river and called Seaman. "We're heading home, boy!" he said, grinning. "Home to biscuits and corn bread and apple pie!"

Seaman barked and raced beside Shannon toward the fort.

"This time next year, I'm going to be watching the trees bud out in the Kentucky sunshine!" Shannon announced.

The captains said farewell to the chief of the neighboring Clatsops and declared that Fort Clatsop, including its rough furniture, belonged to his people now. The captains also tried to bargain for another Indian canoe, but they could not afford the price the Clatsops were asking. Frustrated and eager to get moving, the captains ordered the men to steal a canoe! It was the first time during the whole journey the captains had allowed the Corps to steal from Indians.

The men pushed off their canoes just after midday on March 23. At last, the Corps of Discovery was heading home!

CHAPTER THIRTEEN

N
W ⟶◇⟵ E
S

HEADING HOME

Late March through July, 1806

Seaman splashed into the Columbia River and swam hard. Moving upstream against the strong current was exhausting. When he reached the bank, he hopped out and shook the chilly water off his coat.

Colter called to him from one of the canoes. "Here, Seaman! Come ride with us."

Seaman leaped into the water and caught up with Colter's canoe. "Riding these rapids was a lot more fun last fall, wasn't it?" Colter said as he helped the dog scramble aboard.

All the explorers remembered the thrill of riding the rapids to the coast. Now the men encountered the same rapids, but this time the river was throwing its power against them. They paddled and poled against the swift current. Sometimes, they tied ropes to the canoes and hauled them up the rushing waters. Other times, they had to portage.

The explorers began their homeward journey in early spring. Food supplies were running low, and the salmon hadn't begun their spring run yet. Game animals were skinny and hard to find.

When they left behind the coastal climate, the explorers saw a countryside awakening from winter's snowy grip. Tiny buds sprouted from the tips of tree limbs. Pale green shoots pushed through the damp soil.

The Indians in the Chinook villages were as lean as the game. As the explorers struggled against the Columbia's current, the Chinooks surrounded them. They visited the explorers' camps at night. The explorers were glad to trade with the villagers for meat and roots. But the villagers charged high prices for their food. When the explorers had traveled past these same Chinook villages on their way to the coast, they had resented the high prices these Indians had charged. Now that food was scarce, the Indians' prices were even higher.

The explorers recalled something else about the Chinooks: These Indians had stolen from them. Since the explorers were traveling more slowly now, moving upstream, the Indians had more chances to steal. They took the expedition's iron tools, spoons, food, even clothing.

The thefts became a major issue. On April 8, Seaman's barking alerted the guard to a stranger sneaking into camp. The guard threatened the thief with his gun. When the Indian wouldn't leave, the guard whipped him with a switch.

Although the captains urged the men to control their tempers, they shared the men's frustration. "These Chinooks are constantly hanging about us," Lewis complained one evening. "As soon as we turn our backs, they steal anything they can grab. If anybody ever tried to steal from me like this in the United States, I'd give him a beating he wouldn't forget. The rascal would think twice the next time his fingers got sticky!"

The thieves waited for moments when the explorers were busy. So the captains posted guards to watch the baggage while the men carried the canoes around waterfalls. Seaman stood guard alongside the men. Sometimes the Chinooks would pester the guards by throwing stones at them. Seaman ran up the bank barking at the stone-throwers, but the guards called him back. They needed to keep every eye on the baggage in this country of thieves.

On the evening of April 11, Seaman was running through the woods near camp when three Chinook Indians called him and held out a chunk of dried salmon. Seaman bounded over and sat down, his tail wagging eagerly. The Indians gave him some fish and stroked his fur. Then they began walking briskly through the trees. As they walked, they broke off little pieces of dried fish and fed them to Seaman.

When they were a few hundred yards away from camp, the Indians stopped. One leaned over and stroked the dog's head. Suddenly another Indian wrapped a piece of rope around Seaman's muzzle and pulled it tight so the dog could not bark or bite. At the same time, the third Chinook threw a long rope around Seaman's neck. As soon as Seaman was tied up, the thieves hurried through the woods, pulling the dog behind them.

Seaman jerked his head from side to side to free himself, but the Indians yanked hard on the rope, choking him. When Seaman stiffened his legs and refused to walk, the Indians dragged him along. The harder Seaman struggled, the tighter the rope around his neck became. Seaman was terrified. Although he had been around people all his life, he had never been handled so cruelly.

An Indian trader was leaving the explorers' camp and saw the ambush. He ran back to camp with the news.

Lewis exploded. He immediately sent Colter and two other men after the thieves. "If they don't surrender Seaman at once, fire on them!" he ordered. "This is the last straw. I bet those thieving rascals plan to butcher Seaman for meat!"

The men grabbed their weapons and ran out of camp. They quickly caught up with the thieves. As soon as the Chinooks realized they were being chased, they dropped the ropes and ran off.

While two of the men ran after the Indians, Colter dropped to his knees and pulled the ropes off Seaman's neck and muzzle. Seaman licked Colter's face and then dashed off after the men.

three of this same tribe of villains…stole my dog this evening, and took him to-wards their village…discovering the party in pursuit of them left the dog and fled.

—Journal of Captain Meriwether Lewis, April 11, 1806

"Come back!" Colter called.

Seaman turned and ran to Colter. The other men stopped and wheeled around. "Let's get back to camp with Seaman," Colter said. "There's no telling how many of these scoundrels are lurking around out here, waiting for a chance to grab our dog."

Before they returned, another Indian was caught in camp trying to steal an axe. The captains were furious.

Lewis ordered the axe thief and his companions out of the camp. "Get out! Instantly!" he shouted, his cheeks red and his fists waving. "If you try to steal our property again, we will kill you."

The chief of the nearby Indian village was visiting in camp during all this excitement. Using whatever signs they could, the captains and the chief tried to talk it out. The chief blamed the stealing on a few bad men. The captains tried to explain their anger without insulting the chief. This topic was like dry kindling—with one stray spark, a fire would burst out.

When Colter and the others returned with Seaman, Lewis calmed down. He threw his arms around the dog and let Seaman drench his face with his wet tongue.

"I think you'd better stay here in camp with us, Seaman," Lewis said. "Some of these rascals around here think you're meat free for the taking. If they can get their hands on you, they'll skin you and eat you."

"And they'll use one of the knives they stole from us to do the skinning!" snarled Colter. "I am getting mighty sick of all this stealing." He clenched his fists.

Shannon laid his hand lightly on Colter's shoulder. "What do they say in Kentucky? 'All's well that ends well.' You were able to get Seaman back without any injuries. Leave it at that, my friend."

"Yes, like my pappy always told me," York added, "Keep the food hot, but the temper cool. Or else you eat trouble for your dinner."

The stealing continued. The captains were past patience and desperate to get past this land of thieves. Thinking they could move quicker over land, the captains tried to bargain with local Indians for packhorses. The Indians set high prices and held out, knowing they had the upper hand in the bargain. Finally, the captains agreed to trade their two large metal kettles for two horses. Now the entire Corps of Discovery—more than thirty people— would have only four small kettles for all their cooking. This was the first time the captains had ever traded a kettle, an object precious in the wilderness.

The captains decided to lighten their baggage by leaving behind the heavy canoes. But Lewis was too angry about all the stealing to let the local Indians have the boats, so he ordered the men to set the canoes on fire.

While the canoes were burning, Seaman began to bark. An Indian was discovered in the act of stealing an iron socket from one of the canoe poles! Lewis blew up and gave the thief a beating. He shouted at the other Indians clustered around the camp. "I will shoot the first person who tries to steal anything from us. And," he screamed, "I'll set fire to your houses. We're not afraid to fight, believe me!"

The expedition continued on foot. Seaman ran beside the men, his tail waving in the breezy spring sunshine. He wore his saddlebags, and the men carried packs, but the heaviest loads were packed on the horses. About a month after leaving Fort Clatsop, on April 27, the Corps of Discovery came to an Indian village by the bank of a stream. Seaman smelled the village's large herd of horses. Little curly tailed village dogs ran to greet them, yapping excitedly.

The Indians were Wallawallas, relatives of the Nez Perce. Relieved to be back among Indians they could trust, the explorers made camp near the village.

The Corps spent three days visiting the Wallawalla village. Seaman played chase with the village dogs and watched the captains smoke with the braves. Yellept, the tall, dignified chief of the village, presented Captain Clark with a beautiful white horse. The captains felt they should give Yellept something equally generous, so they presented him with a sword and some ammunition for his guns.

Soon after the explorers arrived in Yellept's village, a woman introduced herself to them. She was a Shoshone, and she could speak with Sacagawea. Seaman sat near the two Indian women as they chatted happily. Sacagawea took Pomp, now fourteen months old, out of the cradleboard so he could play on the ground. Pomp had just learned to walk. He pulled himself up, grabbing onto Seaman's neck fur. Then he steadied himself by keeping one chubby hand on Seaman's fur as he tottered along.

The captains asked both women to translate when they met with Chief Yellept. During one of their meetings, the chief described a shortcut to the western end of the Lolo Trail that would cut about eighty miles of travel off the explorers' journey.

One night, the Wallawallas threw a huge party for the Corps of Discovery. More than a hundred Yakimas came from a nearby village to see the white men. Altogether, more than three hundred people— the explorers, the Yellept villagers, and the visiting Yakimas—enjoyed the celebration.

Cruzatte got out his fiddle, and the Indians formed a large ring around the explorers, who sang and danced to the lively music. York performed his jig to the Indians' smiles and cheers. Excited by the attention, York patted his chest and Seaman raised himself onto his hind legs with his front paws on York's shoulders. York took the dog's front paws and began to dance, but after slobbering York's face with his tongue, Seaman wiggled away. John Colter, who usually kept quiet around strangers, leaped around the circle, doing an acrobatic dance that made the explorers as well as the Indians cheer and clap.

Even little Pomp became one of the entertainers. Captain Clark placed the baby's feet on his own and danced him around the circle. Pomp squealed with delight, and Sacagawea smiled proudly to see her child honored by one of the captains in front of all these people.

Then the Indians began to sing, moving their feet in place around the edge of the circle. Gradually, some of them moved inside the ring and danced with larger, looser movements. They grinned and giggled when some of the explorers tried to imitate their dance steps. The men in the Corps thoroughly enjoyed the celebration.

On April 30, the explorers waved good-bye to the Wallawalla villagers. Following the shortcut described by Chief Yellept, they cut across a bend in the Snake River.

The explorers had been hiking for two days when Seaman darted through the trees, barking a greeting. The men stopped to see who was coming. Some Wallawalla braves were trying to catch up. They were holding a steel trap that had accidentally been left behind at their village.

The captains were astonished. None of the explorers had missed the trap. Clark shook the young men's hands and thanked them.

"What a contrast, William!" Lewis exclaimed. "Those Wallawalla Indians are hospitable, sincere, and honest. But the Chinooks pestered our men, lied, and stole from our camp."

Clark nodded thoughtfully. "The Chinooks and the Wallawallas are both Indians of the West, yet everything about those two tribes is different. Their language, their houses, their values." He smiled. "It's remarkable, Meriwether. These two tribes are as different from each other as our dog, Seaman, is different from a wolf!"

Bidding farewell to the Wallawalla braves, they proceeded on. A few days later, on May 3, Seaman dashed into the underbrush again. He returned shortly with a band of Indians dressed in familiar clothing. They were Nez Perce. The explorers were delighted to see their old friends and followed them to a nearby village. The expedition's supplies were running low, and the men were eager to purchase food.

The Nez Perce food stocks were also running low, and they were reluctant to sell what little they had. Luckily, Captain Clark had earned a reputation as a doctor when the explorers were living near this tribe last fall. At that time, an old man had shown Clark his sore leg, Clark had rubbed some lotion onto it, and the old man had regained his ability to walk after the treatment. As a result, word of Clark's amazing medical skills had spread through the Nez Perce villages. The Indians were so eager for the services of "Doctor" Clark that they were willing to offer some of their precious food as payment!

The explorers settled into camp near the Nez Perce. They felt like they were among old friends. The Indian squaws admired how Pomp had grown. They smiled to see Seaman, the great bear of a dog who had proved so gentle with the village children. They grinned whenever York, the amazing black-skinned man, walked by.

But the sight of the nearby mountains sent chills through the captains' spines. Winter snows had been heavy, and the snow-caps on the huge mountains sparkled white against the sky. The Indians said it would be at least a month before it was possible to cross the Rocky Mountains.

"So we are in a prison, again!" grumbled Charbonneau. "First, we were in the prison of waves at Point Ellice. Then we moved to the prison of rain at Fort Clatsop. Now we are in the prison of snow!"

Even Shannon was too disappointed by the delay to offer a cheerful word. "If this was the last bite of dried fish I ever had to chew for the rest of my life, I would not be the least bit sorry," he declared at supper. He tossed a few pieces of his fish to Seaman, who scrambled to his feet and caught them in midair.

"Mr. Charbonneau," said York, "you remember that sausage you used to make out of buffalo when we were on the plains?"

"Ah, yes," Charbonneau sighed. "The white sausage, *boudin blanc*."

"Mmm, that sure was good eating," York said, closing his eyes to taste the memory.

Seaman padded over to York and nuzzled his fingers. York smoothed the fluffy hair around the dog's ears.

"Remember the buffalo tongue we ate on the Plains?" added Shannon. "If we could get across the mountains now, we'd find the buffalo herds full of calves. That means there'd be veal. You remember how tender veal is? Not like this stringy elk meat."

"Enough talk about food!" ordered Lewis. "We're all disappointed about the delay. We know a feast awaits us on the Plains. But talking about it just makes the appetite sharper. It doesn't melt the snow or shorten the distance we must travel. Patience. That's what we need to concentrate on, patience."

While the Corps of Discovery camped near the Clearwater River, Captain Clark continued to run a medical clinic for the Nez Perce, and the explorers continued to eat the payments for his services. The Indians also paid Clark in horses. In a few weeks, the expedition's herd numbered more than sixty horses.

Although the explorers' hunger was satisfied, they would need a stock of food for their trip across the Rockies. The captains passed out the few trade goods that were left, so each man could try to bargain with the Indians for the best deal in roots.

One day, Colter took Seaman with him on a visit to the Nez Perce village. When they returned to camp, Colter was holding up his pants with one hand. With his other hand, he gripped the neck of a large, lumpy sack that hung over his shoulder. The sack smelled like soil.

"Did the button come off your pants, John?" Shannon asked. The young man was holding a pair of moccasins on his lap, repairing them. "I've got needle and thread right here. I'll sew it back on if you want."

"I don't have the button," Colter said. He held up his coat. All its buttons were missing, too. "I do have a sackful of roots, though."

Shannon looked puzzled.

"The Nez Perce Indians *love* brass buttons!" Colter said merrily. "They think they're almost as beautiful as those blue glass beads that we used to trade. We're out of the blue beads, but we have plenty of brass buttons. They're all over our clothes."

Colter cut strips of elk hide. He sat down on a log and began braiding them into a rope that he could use as a belt. Seaman padded over and laid his big head on Colter's lap. Colter ran a strip of elk across Seaman's whiskers and grinned when the dog twitched his cheeks. "I don't mind tying my pants together if it saves me from starving when we cross the mountains."

As soon as the other explorers heard the news, they cut the buttons off their clothes and headed for the Nez Perce village. Each man traded his buttons for roots. They had their stock of food for the trip across the Rockies. Now they just had to wait for the snow to melt.

"Meriwether, I think our men need something to occupy their time," Clark remarked one evening. "They go out hunting, but game is nearly impossible to find. They've traded everything they can spare. I know they enjoy visiting with the Nez Perce braves, but they still have time on their hands. Too much time becomes a load that weighs down the spirit."

"You're right," Lewis quickly agreed. "The delay weighs heavily on my spirit, even though I have my journal to busy myself with. I have to remind myself daily to be patient."

Lewis looked around the camp. Some of the men were arm wrestling. York was throwing sticks for Seaman to retrieve. Other men lounged by the fire, their feet wiggling nervously. There was so much pent-up energy in camp that the air seemed to vibrate!

"The men are restless and bored," Lewis said. He thought for a few minutes. "What would you think of having a tournament, William? Our men could form one team, and the Nez Perce braves could compete against us. We have plenty of ammunition. We could have a shooting contest."

Clark's face lit up. "That's a fine idea! We could have a bow and arrow competition, too. And footraces."

"We have plenty of horses," Lewis added. "Our men could compete with the braves on horseback, too."

The Indians were as excited about the event as the explorers. The tournament was held on a sunny day in an open field near the village. Older Indian men and the women gathered to watch the contests, wearing their finest clothing, feathers in their hair, and beads around their necks and arms. The children sat in little groups, eager to jump up and carry the braves' weapons or hold onto their horses.

Lewis took Seaman to a shady spot near the edge of the clearing and told him to stay. Seaman settled down on the ground, front legs crossed lazily, his head held high to watch the competitions. The captains came and sat next to him during the footrace. When Colter raced by, Seaman sat up and whined.

"Down, Seaman," Lewis said, stroking his back. "You can run with Colter tomorrow. This is a race for two-legged runners only."

The shooting contest was next, and the explorers took the prize. Captain Lewis became the tournament's champion marksman when he twice hit a mark at a distance of more than two hundred yards. The explorers cheered proudly.

The braves won the bow and arrow competition. They also proved to be the better riders. Even John Colter, the wildest of the white men, couldn't ride a horse as fast as the Nez Perce braves.

"Look at that horseflesh fly! Those braves swoop down a hill faster than an eagle!" Colter whistled as he watched the braves. He was standing near Seaman, and he ruffled the dog's fur. "They ride as naturally as you swim, Seaman. Like they were born on the back of a horse."

The tournament helped pass the time, but as the spring days passed and the mountains still gleamed like a white wall, the explorers became restless again. The captains decided to move their camp closer to the mountains, to Weippe Prairie, the spot where they had camped when they first stumbled out of the Rockies last fall.

They waited until June 15 and then decided it had warmed up enough to risk a crossing. On the first day of travel, the route looked promising. Delicate wildflowers bloomed on the hillsides. But the next day, the captains knew they had started too early. The horses were trudging through snow, their legs sinking deeper with each step. Seaman leaped through the deep snow like a giant, black rabbit. On the seventeenth of June, the explorers found themselves in snowdrifts up to fifteen feet deep on the sunny side of a mountain, and they knew they had to stop. No matter how hungry they were to reach the rich Plains and their own country beyond, no man could rush the Rockies. The captains ordered the men to build a platform on poles and leave some of the supplies on this platform. Then the Corps of Discovery turned back.

The explorers made camp, and Shannon and another man returned to the Indian villages to find guides who could lead the expedition through the mountains. On the twenty-third of June, the men returned with three young Nez Perce braves. The Indians announced the snows had finally melted enough for a crossing. The explorers cheered! With great excitement, the Corps of Discovery began packing.

The expedition set out early the next morning. Each explorer rode a horse and led a packhorse. Seaman jogged alongside the horses into the high country. The sun shone through the trees, but the air was chilly. They blew out clouds of steam with each breath. But by midday, the men had to peel off their outer shirts. Sacagawea took the blanket off her shoulders and draped it across her horse's back.

The group moved steadily until they reached the area where they had left some of the supplies mounted on poles. York and Sacagawea started a fire, and the men opened a box of frozen venison. The group enjoyed a meal of boiled deer meat, but the Nez Perce guides urged them to hurry. They still had hours of travel before they would arrive at a place where there would be grass for the horses to eat.

For six days, the expedition traveled hard. Unlike Old Toby, these guides were sure of the route. With great skill, they led the Corps through the steep, rugged mountains.

When the Corps of Discovery reached the camp they had named Traveler's Rest last fall, both men and horses were tired but still strong. The horses had missed only one day of grazing. The expedition had traveled 156 miles in six days without any major injuries. They had shaved five days off the time it had taken for the westbound crossing of the Rockies.

The explorers spent the first two days of July camping by the Clark River at Traveler's Rest. Their camp was a merry place. When the hunting parties rode back into camp, the men were singing, and Seaman loped along happily with them. Clark spent the lazy evenings teaching Pomp to play pat-a-cake. Seaman settled down beside Lewis's bedroll at night and watched the captain gaze peacefully at the stars, smiling.

The Columbia River's rapids and the Rockies were behind them. Ahead was the rich Plains country. And home.

CHAPTER FOURTEEN

BLACKFEET AND
BAD LUCK

July 3 through August 12, 1806

Seaman paced through the camp at Traveler's Rest as the men laid out supplies and packed boxes. Something was different about the bustle today in camp. Seaman sensed it, and it made him restless.

Early on the morning of July 3, the men loaded their supplies on the horses. But they didn't climb onto the horses and and ride off. Instead, they stood around, shaking hands and slapping backs.

George Shannon knelt down and stroked Seaman's fur. "I'm going to miss you, fellow," he said.

The Corps of Discovery was about to separate into smaller groups to explore different routes home. The captains wanted to report to President Jefferson about the easiest way to cross the continent. Although the Corps of Discovery had reached the Pacific, their westbound trip had been very long. Before returning to the United States, the captains decided to try some shortcuts that the Indians had described to them.

Captain Lewis planned to take some of the explorers on a route that went directly east from Traveler's Rest. His group would begin by going north a short way along the Clark River.

When the river forked, they would turn east and go upstream over the Continental Divide to the Medicine River. Flowing east, the Medicine River would take them to the Missouri River near Great Falls. At Great Falls, Lewis would send some of his men to dig up the caches they had made before they crossed the Rockies and retrieve their canoes. Lewis would take a few scouts to explore the land around the Marias River. If he ran into some of the Blackfoot Indians, he could tell them about their new white father and his hopes for trade and peace. After his scouting trip, Lewis and his group would travel east by canoe on the Missouri River.

Captain Clark's route started south along the Clark River. From there his group would head northeast over the Continental Divide. When they reached the Jefferson River, they would follow it downstream to Three Forks and then turn east. When they reached the Yellowstone River, they would make canoes for traveling downstream (northeast) until the Yellowstone River flowed into the Missouri.

If the plan worked as the captains hoped, the Corps of Discovery would reunite at the junction of the Yellowstone and Missouri Rivers in about a month. Each group would travel separately for nearly a thousand miles.

Before leaving, each captain said farewell to the explorers in the other's group.

Charbonneau's family was assigned to travel with Captain Clark. When Lewis said good-bye, he clasped Sacagawea's hands and looked into her eyes. In a serious voice, he said, "I'm worried about Pomp, Janey. We've never traveled on the Yellowstone River, and we don't know how fast its waters flow. If one of the canoes capsizes...."

Clark put a steady hand on Lewis's shoulder. "We'll all be fine, Meriwether."

Lewis turned to his co-captain and continued, "The Yellowstone River may be swollen with the runoff from the mountain snows, William. Remember how much snow fell last year?" Lewis paused. "Maybe you should take Seaman with your group. In case somebody falls into the river and needs to be pulled to shore."

Seaman whined softly at the sound of his name. He wagged his tail eagerly. Clark smiled at the dog and patted his head.

"We'll be fine, Meriwether," Clark repeated. "All the men will keep an eye on Pomp in rough waters. And yours is the more dangerous route. You'll need Seaman to guard your supplies while you explore the country around the Marias River. That's Blackfoot territory, and we don't know how those Indians will react to white men."

Seaman looked at the captains' faces. Again he whined, unsure about the nervous tone he heard in their voices.

Clark knelt down and let the dog lick his face. "I'll miss you, Seaman." He stroked the dog's fur.

Then he walked over to the men standing near some of the horses. "Good luck, men," he said, shaking each man's hand. "God willing, we will be together again in about a month."

While the captains spoke with the men, Sacagawea sat beside Seaman. She slipped Pomp off her back and let him touch the dog's fur. Seaman licked Pomp's face, then laid a paw on the woman's lap.

York flopped down beside Sacagawea. He picked up Pomp and lightly tossed him in the air. Pomp giggled and kicked his legs.

"In this place, the mountains part from the land," Sacagawea said quietly. "Everywhere I look, the sadness of parting fills my heart."

"Cheer up, Janey," York said. "The captains are just splitting us up to do a little exploring. Our group will be traveling down the Yellowstone River because Captain Clark says that's probably an easier route home. But Captain Lewis and Seaman and the others will catch up with us soon."

Sacagawea sat silently for a minute. Then she looked at York and nodded. "I have also stood in the shadow of these mountains and seen great gladness."

"You'll see great gladness again," York said, and he patted the Indian woman's shoulder. "The captains know what they're doing. The Corps of Discovery will be back together in a few weeks. Then we'll all head downstream for the Mandan and Hidatsa villages."

Seaman rolled onto his back, and York scratched his belly. "I sure am going to miss you, boy," he said. "I'll tell you what—I'll watch out for Captain Clark and Sacagawea and little Pomp. You take care of Captain Lewis."

Seaman scrambled back onto his feet. York held out a stick, and Seaman grabbed it and pulled. Pomp wrapped his chubby hands around the middle of the stick.

"No fair," York said to the baby. "You're trying to help Seaman win!"

The captains called their groups and mounted their horses. Before they began to ride, the men turned to wave. Seaman barked as they separated.

"Godspeed, William!" Lewis shouted, as he led his group north along the Clark river.

"We'll see you at the junction of the Yellowstone and Missouri Rivers," called Clark. "In early August. Be careful, Meriwether!" His group turned south.

～

Lewis started his trip with Seaman, some of the men and horses, and the Nez Perce guides. The Indians stayed with Lewis for one day, to be sure he was on the correct route. Then they said it was time for them to rejoin their people. Lewis thanked the guides before he waved good-bye. The Nez Perce had been good friends to the Corps of Discovery. Without their kindness and knowledge, the explorers might not have survived.

Lewis's group passed a stream on July 5, and the captain named it Seaman Creek in honor of his dog. As their group traveled east along the river, Seaman smelled the familiar odors of game. Beaver lodges dotted the edges of the river. Deer came to the riverbanks to drink. The explorers passed herds of antelope.

On July 7, Seaman went hunting with some of the men, and the hunters wounded a large moose. The moose bellowed, blood spurting from its flank, and bolted into the trees. Suddenly, it stopped and turned to face the hunters. It lowered its antlers and glared at the men, as if it were about to charge. Seaman chased it away.

They proceeded on. The men talked eagerly about reaching buffalo country. Finally, on July 9, one of the hunters brought back a buffalo. Lewis decided to make camp and let his group enjoy a feast of tender buffalo meat.

The next day, Lewis's group came to a herd of buffalo. Seaman sniffed their familiar earthy odor, a mixture of sweaty fur and overturned dirt. The huge buffalo bulls bellowed at the cows, noisily picking their mates. The animals milled around, bumping into each other, pushing and snorting. The bellowing continued all evening and through the night. It was so loud the explorers' horses became skittish. But the men didn't complain. To them, this was the sound of juicy meat ready to be roasted over open fires!

During the evenings, Lewis wrote in his journal by the light of the campfire. He noted that he was "much rejoiced at finding ourselves in the plains of the Missouri which abound with game." Looking out across the grasses swaying in the wind, Lewis remembered the way the western sea looked on a calm day. The grasses rippled like green waves stretching as far as he could see. There were no trees or bushes to break up the line of the horizon. Facing the sea of grass, Lewis felt like a small creature in a vast world.

To Lewis, the Plains stood for plenty. Plenty of grass, plenty of game, plenty of furs. But one part of the plenty made him feel less than poetic—the mosquitoes! Once again the men had to smear their hands and necks with grease to protect themselves from the army of mosquitoes. They stood in the smoke of the fires to be free of the buzzing pests. They slept under netting they carried in their packs.

In spite of the grease and the netting, the men's faces swelled from the mosquito bites. The pests followed poor Seaman, buzzing around his eyes and mouth. Lewis wrote in his journal, "my dog even howls with the torture he experiences from them...they are so numerous that we frequently get them in our thrats as we breath." The hunters complained they could not take aim to shoot because the mosquitoes formed a thick cloud before their eyes!

When Lewis's group reached the roaring, rushing waters of Great Falls, they made camp. On July 16, Lewis gave his group instructions before he began his scouting trip: The men should retrieve the supplies left in the caches last summer and bring back all the canoes. They should carry all the gear around the falls. When they finished, they were to wait by the river, guarding the supplies, until Lewis returned. Lewis chose three of the men and some horses to go with him to explore the Marias River.

Before he left camp, he called Seaman. "I'm going to leave you here at the river, fellow."

Seaman cocked his head as Lewis talked.

Lewis grinned at the alert expression on the dog's face. He knelt and stroked Seaman's head. "Seaman, I need you to guard our camp again," he said, rubbing the thick fur on Seaman's chest.

As soon as Lewis stood up, Seaman scrambled to his feet. "Stay, Seaman," Lewis said. He mounted his horse.

Seaman sat, watching Lewis's face eagerly.

Lewis told the men to keep the dog in camp so he wouldn't follow the horses. Then he and the scouts rode away.

In the days that followed, the men loaded the horses with baggage. They brought back the supplies from the caches and retrieved the canoes. They tied ropes to the canoes so the horses could pull them on makeshift wagons. Seaman and one man stood guard over the baggage as the others rode, leading the packhorses around the waterfalls. This time the portage went quickly, since the men weren't carrying their supplies on foot over the prickly pears. After the portage, they made camp downstream from Great Falls and got the canoes ready to continue traveling.

After the hard work was finished, Seaman padded around camp. He leaped to his feet when he heard the sound of hoofbeats. But the sounds were made by the horses left in camp, not by Lewis returning.

The men repacked the supplies. They hunted. And they worried about their captain's safety. After all, Lewis had gone deep into Blackfoot country with only three men. The Blackfoot Indians were feared by all the Indians who hunted on the Plains—the Shoshones, the Hidatsas, and the Mandans. Perhaps Captain Lewis was in danger. But the men didn't know where he was, so how could they go to his rescue?

Seaman stayed close to John Colter while Lewis was away. When Colter went hunting, Seaman ran beside him. Around the campfire in the evenings, Colter stroked Seaman's fur, and at night, the dog snuggled close to Colter's bedroll. Although Seaman rested his head on his paws and shut his eyes, he was always listening for the sound of hoofbeats. Day after day, Seaman listened. Day after day, there was no sign of Captain Lewis.

Finally, on July 28, nearly two weeks after Lewis had ridden away with the scouting party, Seaman heard the pounding of horses' hooves running hard across the plains. He began to bark and dashed up the riverbank and into the tall grasses. Lewis and his scouts were coming! They were riding swiftly, shouting and waving their hats at the men in camp.

Captain Lewis jumped off his horse and breathlessly greeted Seaman and the men. He knelt to stroke Seaman as he told their story: "We met a party of Blackfoot braves, and they camped with us. When they thought we were asleep, they tried to steal our weapons. They were going to disarm us, then kill us—the scoundrels! As soon as we began to fight them off, they tried to drive away our horses so we'd be stranded."

Lewis and his three companions were breathing hard. They kept glancing nervously back across the plains for any signs of horseback riders.

"What happened?" John Colter asked. "Did you kill the Blackfeet?"

"We killed two of them in the scuffle. So we must hurry," Lewis said. "The other Blackfoot braves have probably gathered a large war party by now."

The men quickly loaded their gear aboard the canoes and pushed off. They paddled hard, trying to put miles of river between their small group and the enraged Blackfeet. Two of the men rode beside the river, herding the group's horses.

Aboard one of the canoes, Colter looked closely at Lewis. "You look worn-out, Captain," he said.

"We rode for a day and a night, only stopping briefly to rest the horses. Then we rode hard all the next day," Lewis explained. He rubbed his neck. "I'm not just worn-out—I've never been so sore in my life!"

That night, the explorers made camp on the far side of the river, just to be sure the Blackfeet could not ambush them in the dark. After posting a heavy guard, Lewis crawled on top of his bedroll. It began to rain, but there was no shelter near the camp. Seaman settled down next to Lewis, and Lewis threw one arm over the dog's warm body. Then he fell into a deep, dreamless sleep. When he awoke in the morning, he and Seaman were both drenched.

Paddling hard, they headed away from Blackfoot territory. The sooner they reached the spot where the Yellowstone River flows into the Missouri River, the sooner they would have all thirty-three members of the Corps as their fighting force. They reached that spot on August 7, but Clark's group was not there. The explorers pulled the canoes onto the banks and searched for signs of the rest of the Corps. They found the ashes of a campfire and footprints. Seaman padded around, sniffing. When he found a pole stuck in the ground, he barked. A note was stuck on top of the pole.

Colter grabbed the note and handed it to Lewis.

"It's from Captain Clark," Lewis announced. "He says they moved their camp downstream because mosquitoes were more plentiful than game at this spot. So we proceed on."

"All right, let's pull those paddles!" called Colter, as he splashed into the river.

Lewis's group kept traveling. Although they found several more notes at abandoned campsites, they couldn't tell how far ahead Clark had led his party.

On August 11, Lewis spotted elk on an island. Since his group was running low on game, he ordered the boats to pull up. Lewis took Seaman and Cruzatte to do some hunting. The two men shot one elk and wounded another. Plunging into the trees after the wounded elk, Lewis spotted the animal, stood up to aim, and was knocked off his feet by a blast.

"I've been shot!" he screamed as pain stabbed through his left thigh. He reached around and felt the seat of his buckskin trousers. The back of his pants was ripped, and when he looked at his hand, he realized he was bleeding heavily. "Cruzatte, where are you? Did you mistake me for the elk, man?"

Cruzatte didn't answer. But Seaman came crashing through the underbrush and sniffed Lewis's wound. Lewis ripped a strip of leather off his shirt and tied it around the seat of his pants to slow the bleeding.

"Come on, boy," he gasped. Using his rifle for support, he limped back toward the boats. As he emerged from the brush, he shouted to the men. "Grab your guns! I've been shot! I think we've been ambushed, and I don't know if it's the Blackfeet. The Indians have Cruzatte!"

The men grabbed their guns and ran into the trees. Lewis limped after them, but his wound had become so painful he could not continue. He slumped to the ground, and Seaman stood guard next to him. Lewis was confused. Why wasn't Seaman chasing after the Indians who attacked him? For that matter, why hadn't Seaman warned him that strangers were nearby?

Soon the men came running back to the riverbank. Cruzatte was with them, and he was unharmed. Nobody had seen any Indians. No footprints, no sounds.

With the men's help, Lewis ripped off his bloody trousers and bathed his wound. Luckily, the shot had not hit a bone or an artery—it was a flesh wound. The rifle ball had passed through the skin on Lewis's left thigh and lodged in his buckskin trousers.

The men argued about how Lewis was shot.

"I didn't see any signs of Indians or any other people," Colter said. "If somebody else was in those woods, we would have seen footprints and snapped twigs. Anyway, Seaman would have warned the captain of an ambush."

Cruzatte kept denying he had fired the ball that hit Lewis. But everybody knew how easy it would have been to mistake a man in leather clothing for an elk, especially with trees and brush to block the view. Since they had no other clues, the men suspected that Cruzatte had accidentally shot his own captain!

Meanwhile, Lewis doctored himself with the help of the men. They carried him to one of the canoes and laid him face down so there was no weight on his wound. Seaman curled up beside Lewis, and the wounded captain held onto the dog so he wouldn't roll as the boat moved. The men paddled hard downstream, hoping to catch up with Captain Clark's group.

That evening, Lewis was in so much pain the men were afraid to move him. So he spent the night lying in the boat. The men soaked cloths in medicine and placed them on his wound. Lewis developed a fever during the night, and he tossed and turned as he dozed. To bring down his fever, the men bathed his forehead with cool water.

Seaman stayed beside Lewis all night. Each time the patient awakened from his restless sleep, Seaman gently licked his face.

The next morning, the group started early. As they paddled down the Missouri River, they met two white men paddling upriver. These were the first white men the explorers had seen since they left Fort Mandan about a year and a half before. Seaman stood in the canoe and watched as the strangers pulled their boat alongside the explorers' canoes.

The men introduced themselves as Joseph Dickson and Forrest Hancock, trappers on their way to the mouth of the Yellowstone River to hunt beavers. The explorers introduced themselves as the men sent by President Jefferson to explore the West. They explained they were in a hurry to rejoin the rest of their group because their captain had been wounded.

"You going to be all right? Do you need any help?" the trappers asked Lewis.

"I think it's just a flesh wound," Lewis said.

The trappers asked about the country upriver, and Lewis offered to give them a copy of the lists of distances that he had used.

"That would be real helpful," Dickson said.

John Colter fished the lists out of Lewis's pack and handed them to the trappers.

As Hancock took the papers, he looked into Colter's eyes and said, "We'd like to take another man with us." The trapper searched the faces of the other men. "How about it? Any of you want to go back up the river?"

Lewis explained that all of the men were enlisted in the Corps of Discovery.

Dickson and Hancock thanked Lewis for the lists. As the explorers started to paddle away, Dickson called to them. "My partner and I have changed our minds. Mind if we stay with your group for a while? Who knows? Maybe one of your men will decide to come out West with us. We sure could use an extra man."

Lewis told the trappers they were welcome to come along. Later that day, the boats rounded a bend, and Seaman stood up, barking happily. The men soon spotted the reason for Seaman's excitement: Captain Clark and the others were in camp alongside the river.

"Captain Lewis is wounded. He was shot!" called the men aboard the canoes.

Clark came running down to the boat. The color drained from his face when he saw his partner lying on the bottom of the boat. "What happened, Meriwether?" he said, shocked.

The others told the story as they carried Lewis into camp. Sacagawea and York heated water to wash the wound and tore cloth for fresh bandages. Clark carefully examined the injury. Then he gently cleaned the area and bandaged it loosely.

"How does it look, William?" Lewis asked. "Has my wound gotten infected?"

"I think it's pretty clean," Clark said. "The skin should heal in a few weeks. The ball ripped out a hunk of your flesh, but it didn't do any serious damage."

"That's a relief," Lewis said. "When the pain became so bad I couldn't walk, I was afraid the injury was worse."

"This is quite a piece of bad luck, though," Clark said, frowning. "We've come all the way back from the Pacific Coast. We're practically at the Mandan villages, and now you've been shot. And by one of our own men, it seems." Clark shook his head. "Well, thank God it's not too serious."

Lewis looked at Clark and grinned. "I guess you won't be able to complain about me sitting around too much!"

Clark broke into a laugh. "No, Meriwether, I dare say you won't be sitting at all for quite some time!"

When Clark finished doctoring Lewis, Sacagawea knelt by the patient's side and gently fed him some broth. The captains recounted the events that happened on their separate routes. Clark was shocked to hear about Lewis's fight with the Blackfeet.

"It's a miracle you weren't wounded—or killed—in that encounter, Meriwether!"

While the captains were talking, Seaman made a quick run through camp to greet the men. When he spotted George Shannon, he ran to the young man. Shannon knelt and scratched Seaman's back and thighs. The dog twisted his head around, his mouth open in what looked like a grin. After a few minutes, Seaman wiggled free and trotted back to Lewis's side.

As soon as Seaman returned to the group gathered around Lewis, York tossed a stick for him to retrieve. But Seaman merely wagged his tail.

"Okay, Seaman, I get it," York said. "No playing games while you've got a patient to look after. Is that it, boy?"

Seaman woofed and nuzzled York's hand.

Later on, Sacagawea took Pomp out of his cradleboard to feed him. Seaman edged close to the baby and nuzzled a soft greeting. Pomp buried his hands in the dog's fur and said, "See-mah!"

Sacagawea paused, surprised. She waited to see if Pomp would repeat the sounds.

Lewis hoisted himself onto an elbow and asked, "Janey, did I just hear Pomp say Seaman's name?"

Sacagawea shrugged. "I don't know," she said.

Seaman gently nudged little Pomp. He bathed the baby's face with his sticky tongue.

The spit-bath made Pomp giggle. He repeated, "See-mah! See-mah!" in a loud voice.

Sacagawea looked at Lewis. "Yes, I think he did say Seaman's name." She smiled proudly.

Lewis laid his head down on his bedroll and sighed. It was a very good feeling to be together again with Clark and the rest of the Corps of Discovery. His wound throbbed, but he was not worried about it. Clark had taken a good look at it and declared it was not serious.

Later that night, Lewis wrote in his journal for the last time on the expedition. He noted that it hurt to hold himself in a position to write. Captain Clark took over the job of recording their journey.

Before he fell asleep, Lewis called Seaman to his side. Stroking the dog's long fur, he reflected on the events of the past month. Near the end of their journey, the expedition had met up with some Blackfeet and some bad luck. But their luck was changing. The Corps of Discovery was all together again. Soon they would be heading home.

CHAPTER FIFTEEN

WILDERNESS
FAREWELL

August, 1806

The reunited Corps of Discovery set out on August 13, 1806. On their second day of travel, Seaman put his front paws on the side of the canoe and gave his greeting bark.

"Hello! Hello!" shouted Clark. He smiled and waved. "We're back! We've returned from the western sea!"

Lewis painfully pushed himself up to see who Seaman and Clark were greeting. Indians stood along the bank. Behind them were the Mandan huts. The villagers ran down to the riverbank to welcome the explorers. They smiled warmly to see their friends returning after such a long trip.

The expedition made camp near the Mandan villages. A stream of Indians came to visit. Captain Lewis could not sit up yet, and his wound was too painful for him to walk much. But he was delighted to be surrounded by the Mandans. It was a homecoming for the explorers.

Around the evening campfire, the captains talked eagerly of the bigger homecoming—their return to the United States. Seaman lay beside Lewis as they talked. The dog's big head rested contentedly on his front paws.

"We have made such quick progress down the Missouri River, William," said Lewis. "I have no doubt we'll reach St. Louis well in advance of winter."

Clark beamed. "Oh, the thought of returning to our country fills me with such joy, Meriwether!"

"I am eager to present the results of our expedition to President Jefferson," Lewis said.

Both captains grew silent, lost in thoughts of the world they had left behind. A world of starched clothes, carpeted floors, and gleaming silverware. A world of refined gentlemen and delicate women. When the captains reentered that world, they would be heroes—the first American citizens to travel across the continent.

Suddenly, a man entered the circle of firelight. Seaman's head popped up, and his tail thumped.

"Begging your pardons, Captains," John Colter said in a quiet voice. "I have a matter I'd like to discuss with you."

"Have a seat, Colter," Clark said cheerfully. "Captain Lewis and I were just talking about our satisfaction at nearing the end of our journey. We expect to arrive in the United States before winter."

...a Croud of the nativs on the bank...were extreamly pleased to See us.

—Journal of Captain William Clark, August 14, 1806

"That's what I came to talk about," Colter said. He sat down facing the fire. Seaman stretched out his front paws and yawned, lifted his rear end, then padded over to Colter. He plopped down in front of Colter and rolled onto his back. Colter grinned and scratched the dog's belly.

"Were you wondering when we will discharge you and the other men?" Clark asked. He glanced at Lewis. "When we reach St. Louis, we'll pay you, and your service to the Corps of Discovery will be finished."

"I figured our service would end once we reached St. Louis," Colter said. He seemed to be struggling to find the right words. "You see, Captain, what I mean to say is...I'd rather not return to St. Louis."

Both captains stared at Colter. He avoided their eyes, looking instead at Seaman.

"Just the thought of St. Louis makes me feel uncomfortable," Colter explained.

"Uncomfortable?" Lewis asked, astonished. "Why, St. Louis is part of your homeland, Colter! It's the doorway to your friends, your family, the world where you were born."

"Well, I've thought about all that," Colter said. "And I guess I feel like I was born to be out here, in the West. In the wilderness. Back there, in the States, I always felt like I was crowded. Like there wasn't enough room for me." Colter paused.

Seaman wiggled closer to Colter. Colter smiled and rubbed the dog's chest. "I guess I felt like a big dog tied up in a tiny little yard when I was back in the States. I reckon Seaman knows what I mean. Out here, I can stretch out my legs and run. It's a fine feeling. I don't want to go back to the States. I'd like to request my discharge here, sirs."

"If you don't come with us to the United States, what will you do?" Clark asked.

"I'd like to go back to the Yellowstone River. To trap beavers with those two fellows, Dickson and Hancock."

The captains' eyes met. Lewis shrugged and nodded.

Clark spoke. "Are you sure that's what you want, Colter? You've been in the wilderness for more than two years. You may feel differently when you get back to your own country. To the country where you belong."

"The West is where I belong," Colter said simply. "I'm sure."

"You've done a fine job for the Corps of Discovery, Colter. You're a strong boatman and a fine hunter." Clark smiled. "You're as brave a man as I've ever met. If you really want to be discharged at this point, you have our approval. And our blessing. Good luck to you, John."

"Thank you, sirs." Colter stood up. "I'll stay with the Corps until you leave the Mandan villages. Then I'll be heading out West." Colter leaned over to stroke Seaman's head. "Sure will miss this dog. Wish I could take him with me to the Yellowstone River."

Colter slipped away, and darkness replaced his spot by the fire. Seaman whined and followed Colter.

"How quickly a man can forget the customs and pleasures of his childhood!" Lewis exclaimed.

Clark shook his head. "I don't think that's it, Meriwether. I think John Colter has discovered the man he really is. In spite of the customs and pleasures of his childhood. He was born to be in the West. It suits him as well as it suits your dog, Seaman."

The next few days were filled with good-byes. The captains paid Charbonneau about five hundred dollars for his and Sacagawea's services. His family would remain at the Mandan villages.

On the day the boats were leaving, the Mandans gathered on the banks of the river. Charbonneau's family and John Colter walked with the explorers down to the boats. Sacagawea slipped Pomp out of his cradleboard so the explorers could say good-bye to him. Pomp walked between the men on his short, fat legs. Seaman darted to the toddler's side, and Pomp grabbed the dog's fur to steady himself.

"He is a beautiful, promising child!" Clark declared. "I would be delighted to raise him as part of my family in the United States. What do you say, Charbonneau? I mean it. I can give him the best education available."

Charbonneau looked at Sacagawea.

She thanked Captain Clark for his generous offer. "You have given great honor to our son. But the child is still a baby. I would like to keep him near me until he is older."

Charbonneau nodded and said, "When Pomp is ready to leave his mother, we would be proud for him to live with your family, Captain Clark."

"Good," said Clark, as he shook Charbonneau's hand. "We will send letters by the traders who use the Missouri River." He clasped both of Sacagawea's hands. Then he picked up Pomp and kissed him on the forehead.

John Colter helped the explorers load the canoes for the trip home. But he left his own gear on the riverbank. The men shook hands with him, slapped his back, and wished him luck.

York chuckled as he said good-bye. "I always said John Colter likes to eat danger for his dinner. Take care of yourself."

Colter smiled. "Don't worry about me, York. You've gotten me spoiled on your cooking. I don't like the taste of danger anymore."

George Shannon clasped Colter's shoulders and said, "Remember how good that Kentucky sunshine feels?"

"The sun shines on the Plains, too," Colter said. "What do you say, Shannon? There's room for more than one Kentucky boy out here."

"Not for me," Shannon said. "I'm planning to trade in my bedroll for some books. I want to study law when we get back to the United States."

Colter nodded, and the two men shook hands.

The explorers piled into the boats and pushed off.

Charbonneau's family stood on the bank of the river. Charbonneau called, "Bon voyage!"

Sacagawea held up little Pomp. He waved his chubby hands and shouted, "See-mah!"

Seaman stood in one of the canoes and barked his farewell. Lewis lay on the bottom of the canoe next to Seaman. As the boats pulled away, the captain was silent, deep in his own thoughts.

Clark called to the people on the bank of the river, "Good-bye, Charbonneau! Good-bye, Janey! Take care of Pomp! Godspeed, Colter!"

The boats started to move downstream, and the people standing on the riverbank looked smaller and smaller. Suddenly, Lewis pulled himself up and grabbed the side of the canoe. "Stop!" he ordered. The explorers looked curiously at their captain. Lewis stroked Seaman's face and said something quietly to the dog.

Clark asked, "What's wrong, Meriwether?"

Seaman licked Lewis's face and nuzzled the captain's ear. The dog looked at the people standing on the shore, then whined softly. Lewis nodded and tapped Seaman's back. Seaman paused, looked at Lewis's face, then leaped into the river and swam to the bank. Barking, he raced toward John Colter. Colter ran to meet the dog and knelt down beside him.

"Take care of him, Colter!" Lewis called in a hoarse voice.

John Colter looked up, confused.

"He was born to be in the West. Like you," Lewis said. "He'd feel crowded back in the States. Out here, there's enough room for him. Room to explore, to be the dog he was meant to be."

Lewis lowered himself painfully to the bottom of the boat. There were tears in his eyes as he said, "Let's go home."

On the shore, Colter put his arm around Seaman's back and stroked the thick fur on his chest. Sacagawea carried Pomp over to Seaman and put the toddler on the ground next to the dog. Pomp giggled and grabbed a fistful of Seaman's fur. Colter, Sacagawea, and Seaman watched the canoes move down the river until they were out of sight. Then Colter stood up and gently handed Pomp to Sacagawea. She smiled at Colter as she took her son.

A big grin spread across Colter's face. His hazel eyes sparkled. "Okay, Seaman," Colter said, looking at his dog. "We're going back out West. We're going to swim and hunt every day. When we get to the Yellowstone River, we've got some more exploring to do."

Seaman was panting lightly, his deep brown eyes eagerly watching Colter's face. When Colter turned to grab his gear, Seaman scrambled to his feet, his tail wagging eagerly.

SeaMan

N
W ✦ E
S

Author's Note

This novel is based on the history of the Lewis and Clark Expedition. All of the characters and major events are true. Since this is historical fiction, I have made up conversations to bring the characters to life. I have also filled in details to create a complete story.

How do people know what happened on the expedition?

Both Lewis and Clark, as well as some of their men, kept journals. Quotations from these journals, with the original spelling and punctuation, are used as captions for this book's illustrations.

What happened after the explorers left the Mandan villages?

The explorers had a quick and uneventful trip to St. Louis. They arrived in September of 1806, and the captains discharged the men in October. The explorers were greeted as long-lost heroes. Dinners and dances were held in their honor. In December, Lewis went to Washington, D.C., to meet with President Jefferson.

After the expedition, both Lewis and Clark moved to St. Louis. Lewis was appointed governor of Louisiana, and Clark became superintendent of Louisiana's Indian affairs. Clark married, and he named his first son Meriwether Lewis Clark. Sacagawea's son Pomp was sent to be educated in Clark's household. Clark eventually gave his slave York his freedom.

George Shannon was part of a group that escorted a Mandan chief home after a meeting with President Jefferson in Washington, D.C. In a battle with an Indian tribe along the Missouri River, Shannon was wounded. He lost his leg because of that wound. Later, Shannon studied law and helped prepare the journals of Lewis and Clark for publication.

John Colter remained in the West as a fur trapper and mountain man. He was the first white man to explore the area that has become Yellowstone National Park.

Remarkably, only one explorer died on the Lewis and Clark expedition. Historians think Sergeant Charles Floyd died of appendicitis, a condition which had no treatment at the time. Floyd would have died even if he had been treated in a hospital by the most skilled doctors of the time!

During the expedition, Lewis and Clark collected samples of animals and plants, minerals, and Indian culture. After the winter at Fort Mandan, the keelboat was loaded with specimens and sent back. The Corps of Discovery brought back more specimens at the end of the expedition. Unfortunately, over the years, many of these objects have been lost or destroyed by fire.

Where can you see what's left of the explorers' collections?

The surviving objects are housed in various museums and collections, but many of them are too fragile for public display. Most of the journals are owned by the American Philosophical Society in Philadelphia. Philadelphia's Academy of Natural Sciences houses most of the surviving plants, now dried and pressed, and a few are on display at their website: *www.acnatsci.org/lewis&clark/*. During the bicentennial celebration of the expedition (2003–2006), an exhibit of many of the objects the explorers used and collected will visit several cities. For information about the expedition, sites along the trail, or this traveling exhibit, write to the Lewis and Clark Trail Heritage Foundation, Inc., P. O. Box 3434, Great Falls, Montana, 59403, or visit their website: *www.lewisandclark.org/*.

What happened to Seaman, Captain Lewis's beloved Newfoundland dog?

Nobody knows! In the thousands of pages of journals and notes that the captains wrote during their expedition, Seaman is mentioned for the last time by Lewis on July 15, 1806 (when he was howling with the torture he experienced from the mosquitoes). Because of this note, we know Seaman was with Captain Lewis's group when the Corps separated for part of the homebound journey.

We don't know if the dog stayed at the river with the men who portaged the supplies (as I have written in this novel) or if Seaman went with Lewis to explore the Marias River country.

How many of the details about Seaman in this novel are true?

Seaman was first mentioned by Lewis on September 11, 1803, when the dog caught squirrels and took them to the men in the boats. Lewis never revealed when or where he purchased Seaman. He did state that he paid twenty dollars for his dog when he wrote about the Indian who offered to buy the dog for three beaver skins.

During the three-year expedition, Seaman was mentioned many times in the journals and notes of Captains Lewis and Clark, as well as in the journal of one of the sergeants in the

Corps of Discovery, John Ordway. (Specifically, the dog was mentioned twenty-eight times by the two captains and six times by Ordway.) Often, all three writers recorded the same incidents—they described the time when the dog was severely bitten by a beaver, the time he chased the buffalo bull out of the sleeping camp, and the time when he was stolen by the Indians on the eastbound trip. The journals portrayed a dog who hunted and retrieved game for the explorers, who barked to warn the men of nearby buffalo and grizzly bears, and who suffered many of the same hardships as the human explorers.

Although we don't know where Seaman came from or what happened to him, we do know the dog was a valuable part of the expedition. Like the two-legged members of the Corps of Discovery, he contributed his talents to the expedition's success. Lewis thought so highly of his dog that he named a creek in his honor—Seaman Creek. The creek, known today as Monture Creek in western Montana, is a northern tributary of the Blackfoot River (called the eastern fork of the Clark River during the Lewis and Clark Expedition).

Seaman, a brave and loyal dog explorer, left his big pawprint on the history of America!

Wingate Downs

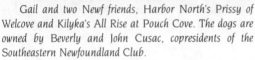

Gail and two Newf friends, Harbor North's Prissy of Welcove and Kilyka's All Rise at Pouch Cove. The dogs are owned by Beverly and John Cusac, copresidents of the Southeastern Newfoundland Club.

About the Author

Gail Langer Karwoski received her B.A. from the University of Massachusetts and her M.A. from the University of Minnesota, later earning her elementary and gifted teaching certificates at the University of Georgia. She has taught elementary, middle, and high school students. Karwoski also coauthored THE TREE THAT OWNS ITSELF, a collection of stories taken from Georgia history. She lives with her family in Oconee County, Georgia.

About the Illustrator

James Watling was born in England and lives in Canada, where he is a professor of Art Education at McGill University. He has illustrated numerous books, including THE CHILDREN OF THE SKY, ALONG THE SANTA FE TRAIL, THE TREE THAT OWNS ITSELF, and THE DEVIL'S HIGHWAY.